THE ORGANICS: CINDER

Topher Kearby

For my family.

TABLE OF CONTENTS:

CHAPTER 1: CLUE

WHATEVER was left of Taurin's youth ended the day the crimson flecks appeared in his eyes. Most people turn their backs on the boy, save for Pulp and Violet, and even his own father, weary from a lifetime of struggle, has little to do with him now. Taurin has been marked without warning or explanation. Hiding among the forest trees that cloak the Temple of Light, he hopes to find out why.

Taurin reaches into his pocket and pulls out a crumpled piece of paper.

It's time to meet. Be at the temple at dusk.

He's read the words a hundred times, and still they haven't changed. So, where is Clue?

Why hadn't Clue shown up himself? He'd been the one who told Taurin where to be and when. Could it be another riddle? Clue had given such short notice this time that if there really was a hidden message, Taurin didn't have time to figure it out.

Clue. It is a fitting name for someone who seems obsessed with hiding the true meaning of his messages. Like when a slab of wood came with a note that read, *Burn bright with flesh. Light the night.* It was by pure accident that Taurin had set the scrap on fire, that he'd become so frustrated flames leapt from his hands. Clue had been leaving Taurin all kinds of things: scraps of wood; three spoiled apples; a swatch of fabric ripped down the center. At first Taurin dismissed them as a joke. But each had proven to be something more.

That's why today's letter is so strange.

Taurin wads the note in a ball and pushes it back into his pocket. For a moment he considers uncovering his speeder and blazing a trail home, leaving behind all of Clue's strange letters and returning to the boring life he had before the crimson flecks had appeared in his eyes.

"Be brave," Taurin mumbles, deciding to move forward. In front of him, slivers of moonlight reveal thick green vines that strangle the temple's stone bricks. Roots, thick and wild, break through nearly every slab of dirt and stone in sight. The Temple of Light looks nothing like its name implies.

Onward still, his woven sandals reach the first step of the winding stairway leading to the temple door. There are nearly twenty more to climb, each cracked and crumbling. Taurin curls his fingers into fists. He's never been in an actual fight before, other than the occasional wrestling match with his brother, Pulp, but if something went wrong, he'd improvise. His long strides carry him to the top of the stairs where a wooden doorway, splintered and rotten, sits directly in front of him. He grabs the metal handle with trembling hands. One quick pull swings it wide.

"Hello?" Taurin whispers. "Anyone here?" Silence. Not a bulb or candle is lit. The dank smell of wilted paper and musky leather fills his nose. *Creepy.*

Trying to concentrate, Taurin looks down at his hand. He's done this before, but never under such pressured circumstances. The lone image of a roaring fire burns in his mind, and within seconds, sparks spring from his palm and grow into dancing flames. "Never gets old," he says, smiling.

Orange light spills into the small room, shining through the darkness. Taurin searches the piles of spoiled books and toppled shelves, but turns up nothing of interest. Then, just as he's about to give up, something strange snags his attention: a pale-blue, almost pulsing light beckons him from across the room. It must have been there all along. Or had it? Inching forward, mindful of his surroundings, Taurin stops as soon as he can see it—a thin glass object resting against a tall stack of books. As long as his hand and twice as wide, it remains entirely transparent except for five strange symbols that shimmer in its center. He's never seen anything like it.

Boom! A rumble, low and full, fills the temple air, vibrating until it rattles deep inside Taurin's bones. Tiny pebbles bounce like insects against cracked tile. Dust shakes loose from the ancient walls.

Watch Force. Taurin couldn't be more certain.

The flame in his hand vanishes, leaving only the blue glow to light the room. Without hesitation, he grabs the pulsing object and throws his body flat against the floor; if he could melt into the cracks, he would. Instead, the boy slithers beneath a stack of dusty books, doing his best to hide. Fiery fists or not, the Watch Force would make quick work of him.

A moment later, a steady yellow beam scans the room inch by inch. A black gloved hand grips tight the polished, metal flashlight from which the light shines. "I could probably take *one*," mumbles Taurin, and for a second fights the urge to rush the dark figure, tackle him against the temple floor, and ignite the soft tissue of his throat. Instead, he swallows a deep gulp of pride; if he couldn't even wrestle Pulp to the ground, how'd he expect to do it to a grown man?

Still, he couldn't just wait around for them to find him. Where there was one patrolman there would be another. Where there were two there would be three. For all Taurin knew, there could be ten. Knowing something must be done, he slides the glass tablet into his leather bag, stretches out his hands, and presses them against the tile floor. "Here goes nothing," he murmurs and squeezes his eyes shut.

Rolling fire fills the boy's mind, bones rattle inside quivering skin, and soon, a thin stream of fire pours from his fingertips. Taurin's eyes open and he can see a burning line snaking toward a stack of splintered shelves. Like a match tossed into a stack of dry leaves, they burst into flames, causing the patrolman to stumble backward.

Firelight exposes the black helmet and visor that covers the intruder's head and face. A red WF is stitched onto what looks like the front pocket of a tailored suit jacket. Pleated pant legs disappear into tall black boots that are laced to just below his knees. Gripped tightly in one hand is the flashlight; the other wields a heat pistol. He isn't here just to look around—he's come for Taurin.

Without hesitation, the patrolman hurries out the entrance of the temple, slamming the door behind him. Taurin doesn't have time to think. Swaying flames become a rampant blaze, inching closer to him with every passing second. The fire was meant to be the boy's ticket to an easy escape. Now it looks like it may be his ruin.

He kicks the wall behind him. Small bits of rock and dust fall and scatter on the floor. The inferno has spread out of control, and if he doesn't act soon, Taurin will be boiled alive. Improvising, he lets loose a flurry of fists that smash against the stacked stone. Blood spills from his knuckles, but he keeps hammering away until the small crack grows into an opening just large enough for him to crawl out of.

He shoves his body through the hole, ripping his gray, cotton shirt on the jagged pieces of rock. Taking a quick breath, he tucks the torn fabric back into his jeans and sprints ahead into the forest. A familiar collection of bent branches and piled leaves remind him when to stop. He can almost feel the growl of his ash speeder beneath the greenery. He brushes off the leaves, moves the branches, and positions the machine upright. It's just as he left it—rusted and beautiful.

Taurin tosses his leg over the seat, fires up the ignition, and twists the throttle all the way forward. Within seconds, his speeder is screaming through the tangled vines and crooked branches of the forest path. These broken-down roadways are said to be cursed, filled with unseen dangers, but Taurin has spent enough time exploring them to know the real threat is the roadways themselves. Normally, he would take the time to navigate them properly, but right now that's a luxury he can't afford. The Watch Force move like ghosts in the night. Nobody knows the reason for their actions because they rarely leave anyone to talk about them. The few who have lived through an encounter keep their mouths shut. If forced to choose, Taurin would prefer to be one of the latter.

Focus, he tells himself. You *can make it home.*

A piercing beam of light explodes in front of him. Blinded, he has no other choice but to slide to a stop. He gulps and places his hand to his chest as his worn rubber tires just miss the splintered tree trunk in front of him.

Taurin thought he knew the best paths through the forest, but maybe he was wrong. The Watch Force found him with ease. Did Clue tip them off? Was he followed? The boy pulls his speeder behind a thick tree trunk and sinks a sandaled foot into the loose dirt; he relaxes the other on the speeder's metal footrest. The Watch Force haven't seen him, and he'd like to keep it that way. One wrong move could cost him everything.

Steam rises from the chrome tail pipes of the six ash speeders blocking the path ahead. The familiar red letters *WF* stand out against the matte black finish of their fuel tanks. If there was any doubt in Taurin's mind who was after him before, there isn't now.

Silence sweeps through the forest. The once-thundering engines are now idle. Taurin peers through the shadows, watching the patrolmen dismount their speeders. Black boots push deep into white ash. Metal rifles press hard against firm shoulders. The patrolmen are hunting on foot.

A metallic taste swims up Taurin's throat, but he gulps it back down and readies himself for action. With the flip of a switch, his speeder's headlight floods the path with light. The patrolmen shield their eyes for only a moment, but it's long enough for him to make his move.

He smashes the throttle forward, spinning the tires and spraying dirt in every direction. His speeder weaves around the hunters and covers them in dust and debris, but to Taurin's surprise, they don't fire a single shot in his direction. Instead, they stand like statues in the middle of the trail and watch as he disappears into the forest. As strange as it may be, he can't help but smile. Had he really met the Watch Force and survived?

"Violet's never going to believe this!" he says.

WATCH FORCE

CHAPTER 2: VIOLET

BACKTRACKING through unmarked roadways, Taurin drives his speeder through the forest shadows, his movements cautious. He'd escaped the temple with his life, but the Watch Force never stop hunting. Days spent tracking wild animals with his father and brother in the untamed parts of Cinder finally proved useful. Taurin spent the last several hours making a series of backtracks and misdirections to confuse the patrolmen and blanket his escape. The effort, while successful so far, has drained him of every last drop of his energy. He needs to rest, if only for a moment.

Just before dawn, as the Cinder sun illuminates the bottom of the night's sky, Taurin steps from his speeder and takes a deep breath. Sweat drips from his forehead. Steam hangs above the speeder's tailpipe.

He moves close to the edge of a towering cliff, his feet covered with ash and wrapped in hand-woven sandals. Each step presses hard into the dry dirt and loose gravel. Like so many places unknown to others in Cinder, Taurin's been here before. The Lookout, his father called it, is a menacing slice of earth, slathered with jagged rocks and scorched of any life. The view, however, is something quite special.

From the top of the cliff, the crumbling boxes of stone that the people of Cinder call homes look refined. Neat rows of concrete houses are divided by thin lines of gravel paths. Smoke rises from the processing plant to the east where his father spent countless hours in the sweltering heat of the factory's refinery. Such is the lot of most who live in Cinder. The processing plant or the mines–both terrible choices, but the only options they have.

"I need to get back," Taurin tells himself. Daylight will soon shine its light on what he's been up to. He tosses his leg over the machine and brings the metal beast back to life with a twist of the rusted key. The dense green of the forest fades and the lines of crumbling stone buildings spring up around him. He was told this place was beautiful once, every window frame filled with painted glass, each door cut from the finest timber. Now, it's just row after row of concrete boxes. Each one more broken than the last.

"Taurin?" A whisper crackles in the air. "You're late!" Violet leans against the side of her own concrete house, hers with a rusted tin roof. Dressed in a purple sweatshirt, she folds her thin arms across her chest to block the chill of the morning air.

The memories of a young girl, hair the color of a raven's wings, eyes like melted chocolate, dance into Taurin's mind. Her small hand is outstretched, holding a lit homemade explosive. "Throw it, I dare you." Violet was different from the first moment Taurin met her; she was special.

She still is.

Taurin steps down from his speeder. "It's been a long night. Just help me stash this, will you?"

"Fine, but you have to tell me everything." She yanks the speeder from Taurin's hands and walks it to a small building behind her house. Placing her palm against the wall, she slides the door open. With one firm shove, the speeder rolls into the shack. She turns, hoping Taurin noticed.

"Am I supposed to be impressed?"

Violet raises one of her thin black eyebrows. "You were *supposed* to be here hours ago." She starts toward the back door of the house and brushes her shoulder against Taurin. Curling her finger, she motions for him to follow. He doesn't hesitate.

Inside the door sits a metal pan filled with clean, clear water. Taurin leans down, removes his sandals, and places his sand-covered feet into the cool liquid. His toes begin to tingle. It feels good—normal.

Violet's hand reaches out in front of her. "What are you waiting for?" She motions for the satchel.

"For this night to be over." He steps out of the water and shakes his feet behind him. His fingers scatter the ash and dust from his hair.

"You're filthy!" She covers her mouth to protect herself from the dust, but it doesn't help. Three dry coughs escape her lips.

"You have no idea." Taurin removes his bag and hands it to her. Then, pressing his shoulders against the back wall, he scratches his back along its uneven concrete. "That feels great," he moans.

Violet sits down at the table next to them, crosses her legs, and cups her hand beneath her chin, her face inches from Taurin's. "I'm ready." A fat wax candle burns on the table, casting a yellow glow upon the room.

"Ready for what?" But even before he says it, he knows. Violet's been waiting, and the anticipation is killing her. "Check the bag," he says.

She rushes to snap open the leather satchel. Instantly, a blue glow colors her face. Looking at Taurin, her eyes teem with curiosity. Taurin nods and Violet turns back to the bag, reaches down, and picks up the thin piece of glass, twisting it from side to side. She turns the tablet in her hands, searching it over. "What is it?" she asks, her brown eyes wide.

Taurin shrugs. "I found it in the temple."

"You *found* it?" Violet's left eyebrow arches again, her teeth gnawing at her inner cheek.

"More or less." Taurin stretches his arms above his head and yawns.

"Did *he* give this to you?"

"There was no he." He yawns again. "Just the Watch Force."

Violet's mouth falls open like a door without a hinge. "No way! You actually saw them?" She scoots toward him, fixing her eyes on his. "Did you take this from them?" The tablet shakes in her hand.

Taurin stretches his arm forward to steady her grip. "Take it easy. I almost died bringing that here."

"Take it easy?" Violet slams a clenched fist down against the table. "You come to *my* house while it's still dark, your clothes fried and smelling like garbage, and you want *me* to take it easy?" After a bit of silence, Violet's color begins to fade. Her eyes move to the floor. "You were supposed to be back hours ago, Taurin. I was worried."

"Things got complicated." He rubs his hand against his throat. "I think I burned down the temple."

Her eyes move to the candle, its wick taller and full of fire. "Flames?"

"More like a river of fire." Taurin rubs his knuckles against the front of his shirt. "It was pretty awesome."

Violet jumps to her feet. "Oh, I wish I could have seen it! Did the Watch Force freak out?"

"Um, not really. I'm not sure they even saw me, but can't we talk more about that later? Let's just deal with this right now." He reaches over and snags the tablet from Violet's lap. "I thought they were looking for me, but then I found this."

"Fine, but I wasn't the one bragging about my *amazing* powers." Violet snatches the tablet from him and looks it over for a few moments. "These symbols look familiar. Each is different from the other, but…" she snaps her head up. "I've got it!" She tosses the glass object onto the table and sprints out of the room. Her bare feet smack hard against the wooden floor. A door creaks in the distance, interrupting an otherwise-silent house. Suddenly, a door slams shut and footsteps slap the ground once more.

"I found it!" Violet squeals. Her body wiggles in the doorway. A small leather book shakes between her fingers. "The symbols are a key." She rushes to the table and grabs the tablet. "Give me your hand."

"What? No way!" Taurin shuffles back and burrows his hands under his armpits.

"Trust me. I would never let anything happen to you."

Taurin pauses for a moment, then nods. His hands relax, and he stretches one arm out to where she can grab it. Pulling him to his feet, Violet's fingers curl around Taurin's wrist. Steady, she lays the tablet against the table and presses his palm flush against the glass. His five fingertips lightly touch the symbols covering the thin tablet, its blue glow replaced with a green light. Words fill the glowing screen, falling like raindrops, and Taurin scans each line, attempting to keep up. After a short time, he stops reading and looks up at Violet. His bright eyes are filled with worry.

"What's wrong?" Violet asks.

"It's a list."

"A *list*?"

Taurin nods. "And my name's on it." He steps back and tosses the tablet into Violet's lap.

She picks it up and studies it. "Relax, it's probably nothing."

"*Probably nothing*? It's a screen filled with names, and I'm on it!" He crosses his arms and paces the small room.

"There are a ton of names on here."

"Yeah, but mine's the only one colored in red. Most of the others names are colored black."

"Like a checklist." Violet glances at the tablet once more, then over to Taurin. "I don't think they were looking for this."

"Then they were looking for me." The boy's eyes narrow; his fingers curl into fists. "Clue was in on it from the beginning!"

"Calm down. You don't know that."

"I know they have my name, and that means…" Suddenly they realize the worst.

"I'm coming with you," Violet tells him.

Taurin doesn't argue.

Violet grips tightly to Taurin's waist, the rumble of the speeder beneath them, her heartbeat buzzing against the curve of his back. Taurin doesn't hear the roar, pays no attention to the jarring of the crumbling roadway beneath. Even the closeness of Violet's body is wasted on him now. His father and brother are in danger. He should have warned them, should have told them what he'd seen.

It's too late, he thinks.

Smoke, gray and thick, climbs the sky in front of him. Bursts of flames crack the shell of the concrete box and paint boils on the top of the tin roof that covers his home. "No. No! NO!" Taurin mashes the breaks and brings the speeder to a violent stop. "Stay here!" He tells Violet, leaping from the still-growling machine.

"You can't go in there!" she says, her eyes wild with fear.

Taurin doesn't look back. His trembling hand stretches toward the door and pushes it open. A fire, growing by the second, burns from the back corner of the room. "Pulp? Dad?" No response. Coughing, he tosses chairs and debris out of his way.

A silhouette slouched against the back wall, catches Taurin's attention. He leaps over a splintered table and rushes to where the figure sits. A black cloth covers a man's motionless head. His limp hands are bound with coarse rope.

"Dad!" Taurin rips off the makeshift mask. "I thought I was too late. I thought…" His father sits rigid and silent. "Dad?" Taurin reaches out and shakes his father by the shoulders, but the man's head, severed at the neck, rolls off his body and lands at the boy's feet.

Darkness.

CHAPTER 3: ECHO

PAIN. Taurin reaches up to grab his skull, trying to stop the throbbing. It's no use. Something wants out—or someone wants in. Either way it's out of his control.

Taurin's eyelids peel open, allowing bright light to pour in. Blinded at first, then the surroundings come into focus.

Where am I?

Trees, bent by the weight of their full branches, bow toward a rushing stream that slices the far-reaching field of green into smaller pieces. The sweet smells of wildflowers and budding plants fill Taurin's nose. His bare toes nestle in the soft grasses beneath them.

"Taurin," a voice calls out.

Taurin turns his head from side to side, scanning the area, but sees nothing more than the burbling stream and the tangled trees of the forest.

"Taurin!" the voice says again, this time with more urgency. "I need your help!"

Taurin presses his fingers against his forehead, forming a visor to shield his face from the rays of the sun. His eyes adjust to the light, revealing a single silhouette standing next to the water.

"Hurry up!"

"I'm coming," Taurin says, sprinting toward the voice. The ground feels loose beneath his feet, colors blur together like wet paint. *Something is off.*

"Where were you, little brother?"

Brother? Taurin's mind scrambles for a moment before his eyes lock on the face before him. "Pulp?"

"Yeah, who'd you think it'd be?"

"I don't know," is all Taurin can say. The person in front of him has the same brown eyes, wide jaw, and almond-colored hair that belong to his older brother, Pulp, but it's all not quite right. "How did you get here?"

Pulp turns, his eyes narrow. "Did you hit your head or something?"

"Maybe? I don't remember."

"You're acting weird. Just go talk to Dad. He'll know what to do."

Taurin swallows hard. "He's here?"

"Of course he's here. Who you think is building the fire? You know, the one you were supposed to be helping with."

"Where is he?" Taurin asks, twisting his body around like a corkscrew. "I need to see him right now. I have to warn him!"

"Calm down," Pulp says, his long arm outstretched, pointing over Taurin's shoulder. "He's over there."

Flames flicker toward the sky, consuming a pile of stacked wood that burns just a few yards from them. A man kneels beside it, coaxing the fire to grow larger, burn hotter. Vibrant blues and reds dance in the darkening sky, coloring the man's face.

I know this fire. I recognize this place.

"Is everything all right?" the man asks, now standing.

The tone of the voice is familiar but distorted somehow. "Dad?" Taurin asks.

"Yes, it's me," the man says, walking closer to them. "Did you help your brother gather the wood?"

"No, I don't think so."

"He hit his head," Pulp says, walking toward the fire with an armload of branches.

"Come here and let me look at you," the man says, his hand waving Taurin over.

Taurin takes several small steps, his eyes searching for clues. Scars ripple along the right side of the man's face. An explosion at the factory had marked his father in this way. His hand reaches out, grabs Taurin's face, and turns it from side to side. Thick callouses from a life of hard labor rake against Taurin's cheeks. "Hmmm."

"What is it?" Taurin asks.

"It's worse than I thought," his dad says, his grip tightening.

"What is?" the boy struggles to ask, his jaw constricted. The man doesn't respond; he just squeezes harder. "Dad, you're hurting me!"

"It's for your own good." His father towers over him now. His face twists and distorts. "Your eyes are poisoned." A second hand reaches for Taurin's neck.

This isn't right. This isn't happening.

His father's coarse palms press hard against his flesh, squeezing the air from his throat. "You're just too dangerous," his father continues.

No. It didn't happen like this. This has to be…

"A dream?" Soft and calm, someone whispers in Taurin's ear.

Taurin turns toward the voice, his eyes frantic and his hands searching his neck for his father's grip but finding nothing. "What's going on?"

"Everything is all right. I promise."

He scans the area again, his eyes wide with panic. The swaying trees and flowing creek have been replaced with total darkness. "Who are you?"

"A friend," the voice continues.

"Is this some kind of sick joke?" Taurin twists his shoulders and looks behind him. "I can't see you."

"Calm yourself. You're safe here."

"Safe? I don't even know where *here* is."

"We don't have much time, so I'll keep it simple. My name is Echo, and I'm here to help."

Taurin sprints in one direction and then another, searching for the source of the voice. His mind, muddled and strained, struggles to make sense of the strange environment. "I have no idea what you are talking about. Quit playing games and let me see you!"

"Please, I must concentrate for this to work, and it's difficult to do that where I am."

"Just tell me what's going on!" Taurin spits.

"Of course," the voice replies, still calm. "I'm what's known as an Organic. I can do things other people can't. One of which is talking to you like this. I think you can relate."

Taurin straightens his shoulders, and his lips tighten.

"Good, then I haven't made a mistake in searching you out. The Watch Force have taken me, along with others with similar skillsets. I'm not sure exactly where they are holding us, but I do know it's not a place where any of us care to be."

"What's that supposed to mean?" Taurin asks.

"Fewer of us remain now than when I first came. Not all here are Organics, but it seems they are attempting to seek out those who are."

"The Watch Force?" An image of the crimson WF stitched on the patrolman's uniform flashes in his mind. "What do they want with you?"

"I'm not sure. They came for me in the dark of the night, ripping me from my bed. Now I'm here. From what I've heard from the others here, my family was most likely killed during my capture."

Silence hangs heavy in the air, making it harder to breathe. "I'm sorry." It's all Taurin can of think to say.

"That's in the past. We need your help in the present. Every day, more of those gathered here leave this room and never return. It won't be long until I don't come back either."

Taurin chews on his already ragged thumbnail as he's always done when agitated. "This is just too cryptic. I don't know you, and even if I did, you won't tell me where you are. It sounds more like a trap than a rescue."

"It's not a trap. I can prove it."

A sharp, pulsing pain, pierces Taurin's mind again. The image of a tall boy slumped against a gray wall flickers before his eyes. Rusted chains cuff the boy's wrists, and smears of blood stain his white cotton shirt. A metal sign hangs above his head; the words *Taurin Gray* are etched on its front.

"Who's that? Because it's not me!" Taurin looks closer at the boy. His face, though puffy from bruising, is one he knows well. "Pulp!"

"Yes, they have your brother," Echo says. She pauses before continuing. "They think he is you."

Taurin rakes his hands over his face, clawing his cheeks with his fingernails. "This is my fault."

"No, it isn't. The Watch Force do as they please. You couldn't have known."

"I should've been there!"

"Then you would be here and your brother would be dead. That wouldn't help anyone. Be thankful he is still alive. It's more than most here can say about their families."

Taurin swallows hard and tries to steady his wild breathing. "What do you need me to do?"

"Talk to Violet's father, Brooks. He will know how best to advise you. You must hurry."

"Brooks?" Taurin shakes his head. "That doesn't make any sense. What could he possibly know about any of this?"

"You'll have to trust me."

"What choice do I have? Just get me out of here."

"Of course."

A bright flash of light erases the darkness. Taurin, his face flat against the floor, wakes to the sight of his burning home. The pungent smells of smoke and fire fill his nose. Flames cover every wall of the little house, leaving only a small path to the door. Taurin presses his palms against the floor and stands to look back at his father's body. "I'm sorry."

Sprinting, Taurin hurdles burning piles of his family's possessions and makes his way out of the house again.

"Taurin!" Violet shouts, running toward him. "I'm sorry. I tried to pull you out, but the fire was too much."

"I'm fine," Taurin says, breathless. He presses his hand against Violet's shoulder and sucks in deep gasps of fresh air. "We need to talk to your dad."

"My dad? What are you talking about?"

"I'll explain later," he says, slinging his leg over the speeder and turning the key. The engine rumbles and dust powders the sky from the force of the exhaust. "Hop on."

Violet doesn't hesitate. She climbs onto the speeder and presses her body against Taurin's, wrapping her slender arms around his waist. Within seconds the two are speeding down the dirt path toward her home. For a few minutes while the fire raged, Violet had been sure that Taurin would be lost, and there was nothing she could have done about it. She had never felt so helpless or afraid, and she never wanted to experience those feelings again. She squeezes him tighter.

Maybe if the stark image of his bloodied brother chained to a cement wall wasn't torturing him, Taurin would feel Violet's embrace, but seeing Pulp's bruised body isn't an easy sight to forget. *Was it just a nightmare? A terrible dream?* Taurin shakes his head. He doesn't have the luxury to decide if it's real or not. Time is running out, and Brooks is the only one who might be able to help.

When they reach Violet's house, Taurin rolls the speeder's rubber tires to a stop. The engine falls quiet.

Bam! Bam! Bam! The boy's curled fist slams against the wooden door. *Bam! Bam! Bam!*

"Go away!" a voice shouts from inside the house. "We don't want any trouble."

"Too late for that," Taurin says. "Let me in."

The door swings wide, revealing a tall man with patches of gray hair covering his face and head. A pair of thick reading glasses perch on his nose, and a red bathrobe, rife with rips and tears, covers his body. One of his hands grips a twisted wooden cane. The other holds a heat pistol, the short barrel pointed at the Taurin's head. "I said we don't want any…"

"Daddy, put the gun away. It's just us," Violet says, stepping in front of Taurin.

"Oh, darling, I didn't realize you left. I've been immersed in my own thoughts for hours. What trouble have you two found now? You know it's dangerous out there after dark," Brooks says, holstering the pistol.

"I saw my father's head roll off his shoulders and my brother chained to a prison wall. Some strange voice talked to me through a dream and told me you would be able to help," Taurin says, fixing his eyes on Violet as she gasps and clamps her hand over her mouth at his revelation. Then he turns his attention to her father. "Brooks, quit stalling and tell me what's going on."

The man's head dips to the side. His gray eyes narrow, studying Taurin as if for the first time. "Are you sure you want to know?" Brooks asks. "Once a secret is spoken, it can't be untold."

"I'm sure."

"Very well," he says, pulling a small, clear object from his pocket. "Follow me."

CHAPTER 4: SECRETS

A RED LINE of light traces the shape of Brooks's widespread fingers, then flashes green. The wall, covered with worn wooden paneling, slides to one side. "After you," he says, his arm sweeping Taurin toward the doorway.

The boy takes a step back, shaken. "You can't be serious."

Brooks's eyes, grayed with age, fix on Taurin. "My apologies," he says. "I was unaware you were afraid of the dark."

"I'm not afraid, it's just that…"

Violet stretches her arms into the room and waves her hands in the air. The ceiling hisses to life, flooding the room with light. "He's just messing with you," she says, patting Taurin on the back.

"Oh, you love to spoil my fun," Brooks says, following his daughter into the room. "I merely wanted to see how long it would take him to figure it out."

Blood flushes Taurin's face. "I'm not here to play games."

"Of course, forgive my wandering mind." Brooks motions toward a couch wrapped in white plastic, placed in the center of the room. "Please, sit down."

Taurin's brow furrows and he folds his arms across his chest. "I'll stand."

"Very well," Brooks says, walking to one edge of the square room. "Would either of you like a glass of water, or perhaps something a little more exotic?" The aged man reaches for a potbellied bottle; a thin layer of dust coats the green glass that houses a thick, yellow liquid. Brooks grabs the container and places it on a dark wooden table in front of the couch. With shaking hands, he moves three octagon-shaped tumblers to the table's center and fills each glass with an even amount of the liquid. "Go on. Take one."

Violet leans over, wraps her hand around one of the tumblers, and brings it to her nose. "Gross!" she blurts, pulling her head away from the glass. "What is this stuff?"

"It's from the Wasteland, my dear. I'm told, though pungent, it's quite delicious."

"You haven't tried it?" Taurin asks, grabbing the remaining drink from the table.

"I was saving it for a special occasion." Brooks's thin lips stretch into a flat smile. "Tonight will have to do."

Violet raises the tumbler to her mouth, a finger and thumb clamp her nostrils closed, and pours the gooey liquid down her throat in one large gulp. Her eyes flash open and a shiver shakes her body, but then she traces her tongue across the outline of her thin, rose-colored lips, attempting to capture the last few yellow drops. "Weird...but good."

"Well done, my darling," Brooks says before he too places his glass to his lips and empties it in one motion. His mouth puckers before it springs wide-open. "Delicious."

Taurin studies his drink for a second before he too presses the tumbler against his lips and tilts it back. The liquid, thick and pungent like soured milk, slides across his tongue and drips down his throat. Small hairs spring to attention on his sunbaked arms and make his eyelids flutter. "Hard to believe from the smell, but once it hit my lips everything changed. My face turned warm, my fingers tingled, and a sweet flavor coated my mouth. Incredible."

A satisfied smile curls Brooks's face. "Would you like another?"

Taurin shakes his head and sets his glass on the table. "One's plenty."

"Yes, I suppose you sought me out for what I know and not for my exceptional refreshments."

"Yeah, about that," Violet says, focusing on Taurin. "What made the voice from your dream think my dad could help you?"

"It's a long story and…"

"Yes, yes, you don't have the time. Details of why you came are unnecessary. You are here now, so let's get to it." Brooks shuffles over to Taurin. "Hold out your hand, son."

Taurin stretches his upturned palm toward the old man. Brooks drops a clear cube, no larger than a silver coin, into Taurin's outstretched hand. "What's this?" Taurin asks.

"Be patient," Brooks says, his gaze fixed on the object. "It may take a moment or two."

"This is weird, Dad," Violet says, placing her hands on her hips. "Even for you."

"Um, something is happening," Taurin says. He motions to the coin-sized cube, his eyes wild.

"Just as I expected." Brooks rushes to a metal workbench pressed against the rear wall of the room. He rakes a pile of papers and supplies off the bench, sending the clutter crashing to the floor. "Ah, here it is," he says, reaching for a notebook no larger than his hand. Its cracked leather binding squeezes a stack of yellowed parchments together. Each shred of paper is filled with lines of handwritten notes. Brooks's weathered fingers flip through the worn, dog-eared pages. "I know it's here. Let me see."

"You need to see this," Taurin says, his words slow. A crimson light beams from the center of the once-clear cube and paints his face. "Is this supposed to be happening?"

Brooks rips a single page from his notebook and shuffles back to Taurin. "Don't be alarmed. Things are exactly as they should be. Let me just check my notes for a second."

"Hurry," Taurin complains. "This thing is heating up!"

Brooks's eyes, cool and steady, turn toward Taurin. "How long have you known?"

"What are you talking about? This thing is burning me!"

"That thing is a bit of technology I created. It's meant to reveal what some people wish to hide."

"Daddy, stop this," Violet pleads. "You're hurting him!"

"I didn't come here so you could experiment on me."

"No, you came here seeking my help at the cost of bringing violence to my door and placing my daughter and me in serious danger." Brooks places both his hands on Taurin's shoulders. "Tell me, what are you hiding?"

"Nothing. I swear." Hot tears stream down Taurin's cheeks. "Just get this thing off me."

Brooks moves his face closer to Taurin's. His hot breath falls against the boy's wet face. "Don't know or don't wish to reveal who you really are?"

"Ahhh!" Taurin shrieks with pain. "It's burning!"

"Then make it stop," Brooks says, stepping back. "You are the only one who can."

"Violet, you have to do something! He's crazy!" Taurin cries.

"She can't help you, and the cube can't hurt you unless you allow it to. It's only a tool. Use your anger at me to stop the fire that is burning your skin."

The foul smell of scorched flesh floods Taurin's nostrils. "It's melting my hand," he pleads.

"Concentrate." Brooks fixes his eyes on the glowing cube. "You must control it."

Violet scrambles to Taurin and sets her hand on his back. "I'm sorry," she whispers. "I didn't know this would happen, but I know you can do this."

Taurin clamps his quivering eyelids shut, blocking everything and everyone out. *Be strong. Concentrate.*

"That's it, son. Stay focused," Brooks says.

Taurin leans back and snaps his arm forward. "LET GO!" he yells. The cube sails across the room and smashes against the stone wall. Slivers of clear shrapnel fall from the ceiling like flakes of ash.

"Remarkable," Brooks says and leans down to examine the shattered cube. "This is more than I expected. Much, much more."

Violet's soft hands press against Taurin's shoulders. "You okay?" she asks.

Taurin holds his hand in front of his face, rolling it from side to side. "I can't believe it."

"Believe what?"

"My hand. It's fine. Not even a little charred."

Violet leans in to get a closer look. "Can I?"

Taurin shrugs. "Go ahead."

Violet presses her index finger against his hand and traces his palm. "Not even a little warm."

"Of course not," Brooks says, his loud voice startling the pair. "This boy is a powerful Organic. Just as I suspected." The old man reaches inside a drawer and pulls out a piece of folded yellow paper.

Taurin takes a step back, his hands spread wide in front of his body. "I'm not interested in doing that again. So just put whatever that is back in the bag."

"I'm simply trying to discover the truth. Please, sit down. Both of you." He gestures to the white couch. "I need to show you something very important."

The plastic-wrapped couch cracks and squeaks as Taurin sits down next to Violet. "No more surprises."

"Do you recognize this?" A red *WF* painted against a black background dangles from Brooks's fingers.

Taurin's back stiffens. "*Watch Force.*"

"So, you have seen them? I thought as much, but was skeptical. Few people live to speak of them."

"Like my father?"

Brooks looks to the floor. "I'm sorry. He was a good man."

"Just tell me what you know."

"Yes, of course." The old man flips through the pages of another one of his journals. "The Watch Force do as they please because they can. They've been doing so for longer than you or I have been alive. The Seer has given them that power."

"Who?" Taurin asks.

"Certainly you've heard of the Seer," Brooks says, raising an eyebrow.

Taurin shakes his head. "Not really."

"Well, he's a powerful man who has ruled this land for a very long time. His influence reaches to all corners of Cinder. Perhaps even beyond."

"What's he have to do with me?"

"Excellent question," Brooks says, handing Taurin the journal. "Look at this."

Taurin scans the page, "It's the same."

"The same as what?" Violet asks, impatient. "Why do I feel like the only one who doesn't know what's going on here?"

"How did you get this?" Taurin asks.

"That's not important," Brooks says. "Just know that the others and I are concerned about your fate."

"Others?" Violet asks. Her face twists with frustration. "Seriously, someone needs to…"

Brooks waves his daughter away with his hand. "Not now, darling; you must be patient."

"Who's this?" Taurin presses his finger against the paper. "This name wasn't on the other list."

Violet slides across the cushions to Taurin and pulls the journal from his hands. "I'm done being patient. Let me see that." Her eyes bounce back and forth, searching the page. "Shrift?"

"Well done." Brooks, now holding his tumbler, pours himself another helping of the yellow liquid. "The Seer keeps track of the Organics, but he's not aware of this one."

"And you are?" Taurin asks.

Brooks sips his drink. "Yes, but only by reputation. No one has seen him for quite some time, and I believe he wishes to keep it that way."

"How does any of this help me find my brother?"

"We need to find Shrift," Violet answers.

"I'm afraid there is no we, my dear. Only the boy can make the trip to the Wasteland. It's much too dangerous for a young girl or even a man of my age to make the trip."

"Daddy, you can't expect him to…"

Taurin stands. "Just tell me where to find this Shrift. Whoever he is."

"He's like you." Brooks hooks the straps of a brown, leather satchel over Taurin's arms. "And he's the only one who might know where they are holding your brother."

"What's in the bag?"

"Supplies for your journey." Brooks leans in to whisper. "Not everything in there is legal, so be careful."

Taurin nods. "Just one last thing."

"Yes, what is it?" Brooks asks.

Taurin reaches out and takes hold of Violet's hand. "She's coming with me."

CHAPTER 5: THE FOREST

WARM, wet tears stream down Violet's cheeks. It's not the wind or the dust that is making her cry; it's a hidden truth. Violet wraps her arms around Taurin's waist, squeezing him, assuring the boy that she's still with him. The Wasteland is still far from here, and she knows Taurin will need her to be strong. *There will be time to tell him everything about who she really is, but not right now.*

Taurin turns his head back for a moment. "You okay?"

"I'm good," Violet says, nodding.

He can feel her thin, strong arms wrap themselves tighter around his waist. Her warm breaths falling against the back of his neck cause him to shiver. More words aren't necessary. Violet has his back—he doesn't need to hear her say it.

Sun-bleached, dirt roadways fade to lush paths, thick with tall grasses. Most of Cinder is desolate, scorched by the volcanoes to the north, but the south is green with life. Massive trees with trunks the width of small buildings and bright budding plants, ripe with color, edge the sides of the roadway. Taurin's eyes shimmer at the sight. He's been here before, but now everything seems more stunning.

Pop! Pow! Taurin looks back, the beauty of the moment smeared by the black smoke pouring from the speeder's engine. "Great," he says, rolling his eyes.

"What happened?" Violet asks, waving the smoke away with her hand.

Taurin shrugs. "No idea." He mashes the breaks without warning, bringing the wounded machine to a dead stop and letting the engine idle. Violet's head smacks against his back, dizzying her vision for a few moments.

"You could have warned me!" she says, slamming her fist against Taurin's shoulder.

He winces, his cheeks flushed with embarrassment. "Sorry, I wasn't thinking. You okay?"

A strip of red stretches across the girl's forehead. "I'm fine," she says, rubbing the area with her hand. "You just surprised me."

Taurin hops off the speeder and offers his hand to Violet. She quickly shakes her head and scowls, letting him know that she doesn't appreciate the gesture. "I'm fine," Violet repeats, sliding off the back of the machine.

He raises his hands in surrender. "Look, I'm really sorry. It was an accident."

"Just fix the speeder so we can get out of here. This place creeps me out."

Taurin shakes his head and turns the metal key, silencing the engine and cutting off the belching smoke. His eyes, intense and focused, scan the speeder. Taurin knows every inch of his high-speed machine; he built it himself. But the heat radiating from the engine blocks him from searching for the problem. "It needs to cool down."

"Terrific. It's going to be dark soon, and we're stuck in the middle of nowhere!" Violet grumbles, rubbing her still-sore head with her fingers.

"I get it, you're mad; but none of this is my fault."

"Did you build this pile of junk?"

"Yeah…"

"Did you tune it up before we left?"

"No, but …"

Violet cocks her head to one side, her eyes narrowing. "I came with you because I trusted you."

"No, you came with me because you wanted an adventure. This is just part of it!"

"Being stuck in the forest at night isn't an adventure. It's a death wish!"

A faded memory from one of his trips with his father springs into Taurin's mind: Teeth dripping with saliva, eyes filled with fury, and a sharpened stick plunged deep into the belly of a hungry beast. Violet should be afraid. The forest, though beautiful by day, fills with dangers when the sun sets.

"We'll be fine," Taurin says, pushing the memory from his thoughts. "I came here a lot when I was kid."

"You came to the forest?"

"It's no big deal. Just help me with this," Taurin says, motioning to the speeder.

A million questions rattle in Violet's mind, but the sun is setting and the cooling air bristles her skin. In her haste to leave, she didn't think to grab a jacket or a pair of pants; instead, the thin purple fabric of her T-shirt and the faded jean shorts she'd put on earlier will have to protect her from the elements. Questions will have to wait. "Fine, what do you want me to do?"

Taurin points to a thick patch of trees to the right of the roadway, their twisted branches reaching toward the setting sun. "We need to get the speeder in there."

"Why can't we just leave it here?"

Taurin rolls his eyes. "The Watch Force haven't given up their search yet, so a broken-down speeder might give them a clue where we are," he snaps.

"You don't have to be a jerk about it," Violet says, grabbing the handlebars.

"I was just …"

"Just help me push."

Taurin sucks in a long breath, filling his lungs with the cool air. He closes his eyes, his thin eyelids covering his dry eyes for a moment, then opens them again. His hands, covered with dust and cracked from the heat, grip the speeder's seat. "Ready?"

Violet nods anxiously. Then together, they shove the machine off the path and into the forest. "How far do we need to go?"

"As far as we can," Taurin replies, sweat dripping from his brow. Much like the path to the temple, this area has changed over time too. The trees look wilder, slathered with moss and hanging vines. Once-small patches of wildflowers and grasses have grown to climbing stocks of thorny weeds and vegetation. What looked lovely just minutes ago has morphed into something menacing in the fading light.

Branches scrape Violet's body, but she keeps pressing forward. Taurin's talk of the Watch Force stirs her stomach, pulling her deeper into the darkening wooded area. Her father's nighttime stories often included wild creatures that lived among these tall trees. She loved those tales, mostly because she was always the young girl who saved the day. This, however, isn't happy fiction. The patrolmen that search the roadways won't vanish once she closes her eyes.

"This is good," Taurin says, his voice jarring her from her thoughts.

"You sure?" she asks, her eyes sweeping her surroundings. "Have we gone far enough?"

"I'm exhausted, so it will have to do."

Violet lets go of the speeder, allowing Taurin to lean it against the rough, gray bark of a nearby tree. A canopy of branches, dense with broad green leaves, block whatever light is left in the sky. "It's so dark," Violet says, her small hands rubbing the exposed skin of her arms. "And cold."

"Let me see what I can do about that," Taurin says, and for the first time in hours, a smile grows on his windblown face. He gathers some small sticks and dry leaves and then places them in a pile on the ground; he's gathered such materials before, but this time he doesn't need a match to light them. "Ready?"

Violet nods, still rubbing her shaking arms.

Taurin crouches, his eyes level with the small stack of kindling. A line of shimmering crimson colors a circle around his pupils. "Burn," he says. As if the pile of debris had been soaked in fuel and lit with a match, it ignites, spilling a warm, orange light over an area just large enough to cover the two young travelers.

"Show-off," Violet says. She smiles and sits down next to the fire. Her flittering fingers reaching for the flames' heat. "It's easy for you not to be afraid when you can do that."

Taurin drops down next to her, letting the heat from the flames roll over him like a warm blanket. "Honestly, I'd be freaked if it were just me." His eyes, now deep blue and littered with flecks of crimson, lock on hers. "I'm glad you're here."

Violet's chocolate eyes sparkle in the firelight, as her fingers pull long strands of straight raven hair behind her ear. "A lot of good I'm doing you," she says, looking away. "I feel like I'm just added weight on the back of your speeder."

"Oh, you don't weigh that much," Taurin says, nudging her with his elbow.

"You're hilarious." Violet's eyes lost in the canopy above them. The bright green of the forest glistens from the orange and red flames dancing below.

Taurin scoots closer to her, his hand brushing against her leg. "We'll be okay," he says, his voice sturdy. "I won't let anything happen to you. I promise."

Violet looks from the trees to Taurin's face. His touch stirs something inside of her, a warmth and a comfort that she's never felt before. Taurin's been more of a brother to her than anything else, but now, in the middle of the worst place she's ever been, he looks different. His eyes, freckled with crimson, seem strong and reassuring. His familiar fingers press against her leg, but they feel different too, somehow pulling her close to him. *I want to kiss him*, she thinks.

Then she sees it.

"Taurin," she says, her mouth suddenly rigid.

"What is it?" he asks, his face leaning close to hers.

Eyes, yellow and glowing, shine through the darkness just steps behind Taurin. Hot breaths linger like bursts of steam in the air. Violet whispers, "Don't move."

The hair on Taurin's arms stands on end. He can't see what's behind him, but the fear painted on Violet's face explains the danger. A guttural growl rumbles through the air, crawling up Taurin's spine. He quivers. The memory of jagged teeth tearing into his father's leg years ago flashes in his mind.

"Run!" he shouts, pulling Violet up behind him. She doesn't hesitate, and together they sprint into the forest.

"This is crazy!" Violet yells, jumping over a pile of splintered, tangled fallen limbs. "That thing will tear us apart!"

"Just keep moving!"

A violent roar shakes the forest, shaking branches and leaves. The beast's heavy paws slam against the dirt. It sounds hungry.

"Get ready to jump!" Taurin shouts.

"What are you talking about?"

"There!" He points to a ravine just ahead. "It's the only way."

"You're crazy! We can't make that!"

"We don't have a choice!"

Razor-sharp rocks litter the bottom of the gulley, filling a distance longer than four speeders pressed together end to end, and deeper than the forest's tallest tree. The body of a forest deer lies lifeless below them in the valley, its back broken, legs pierced by the stones.

"You can use your powers, right?" Violet asks, her head snapping back toward the beast. Its wild eyes in the shadows grow closer with every second.

Taurin looks at her, his crimson flecks burning bright in his eyes. "I hope so!"

"Perfect," Violet says, her fingernails digging deep into the boy's palms. "Eaten by a monster or skewered on a jagged rock. It's not exactly how I pictured this night."

Taurin squeezes her hand. "I can't do this without you."

Violet bites her bottom lip and fixes her sight on the large gully drawing closer by the second. "Let's do this!"

Without missing a step, Taurin sweeps Violet into his arms and tosses her over his shoulder. Her chin buries deep into his back, the tips of her dark hair brush against the dirt path.

"Hold on!" Taurin shouts, sprinting toward the edge of the ravine.

Violet presses her face flush against the back of Taurin's shirt, her thin legs draped over his boney shoulder.

A vicious roar pulses through the air, giving Taurin the last bit of motivation he needs.

She's counting on you. JUMP!

BEAST
McSKILLERN
'15

CHAPTER 6: QUESTIONS

THE GRASS is wet against Violet's cheeks, chilling her narrow frame. Her shorts and T-shirt offer no resistance to the cool wind rolling over her tanned skin. A veined leaf a few inches longer than her body and half as wide, is Violet's only shelter tonight. The leap over the canyon stole what was left of Taurin's magic, or whatever he wants to call it, so no fire remains in his fingertips. No flames. No heat. Just the cold, damp green of the jungle and the rough branch of a giant fern comfort her.

And, of course, there's Taurin.

Violet's eyes move up and down his body. His arms, smeared with mud and splattered with fresh blood from the fall, curl under his head. Yellow moonlight falls against his face, highlighting his sharp jaw and broad cheekbones. Like lean snakes squeezing their prey, lines of muscle rope his biceps and lower arms. The scrawny boy she's known her entire life has changed.

Without thinking, she spreads her fingers and brushes her hand against him.

"What is it?" Taurin asks, his eyes slow to open.

Violet smacks her hand against his arm, the sound cracking like a leather whip. "Got it," she says.

"Ouch!" Taurin winces. "What was that for?"

"Spider," she says, pulling her hand away. "You're welcome." She turns her head, hiding the red coloring flushing her cheeks.

"I save your life and you beat me up?" Taurin says, rubbing his arm. "Next time I'll just let the monster eat you." A sly smile grows on his face.

"You're hilarious." Violet crosses her arms. "Do you realize how close we were to being that thing's dinner tonight?"

"Relax," Taurin says, sitting up. "I had everything in control."

"Oh, really? Then why were you so freaked before we jumped?"

"I wasn't freaked! I just …"

"You just what?"

"Forget it," Taurin says, looking away.

Violet's hand, small and warm, presses against his wrist. Her red lips open just wide enough for a small whisper to escape. "You just what?"

Taurin looks back toward her, her eyes soft and welcoming. "I just didn't want to lose you," he says, his hand falling against hers. "You're all I have left."

A silent moment hangs in the air like a leaf gliding to the ground. Violet searches her mind for the right words to reassure him in some way. *Just tell him the truth*, she thinks. Instead, she pulls her hand away from his. "We're both tired."

Hurt, Taurin looks down at his empty hand. For a few seconds, he thought there might be something, a spark, between him and Violet. *Stupid*, he tells himself.

"Let's just get some sleep," Violet says.

"I was sleeping before you smacked me."

"Now you can get back to it," Violet says, lying down next to him. Her right cheek presses against a patch of dank greens once again. "Get your rest."

"Good idea," he mumbles before he too lies down against the cool ground. His face rests just inches from Violet's long, wild hair, which spills across the ground like a black river. If he could just tell her how he feels, how he's always felt about her, things would surely be different. Instead, he lets his heavy eyelids cover his tired eyes, replacing the dark night with the silence of sleep.

Then, like a flash of lightning, Taurin is jolted from his rest. No longer lying down, Taurin finds himself kneeling in front of an expansive body of water. The surface of the lake sparkles under the intense glow of the sun, reflecting the deep-blue coloring of his eyes. He cups his hands, which are covered with mud, and dips them deep into the cool water. Taurin doesn't mind the grime; his lips are dry and thick gulps of the liquid soothe the painful thirst in his throat.

What time is it? How long did I sleep? he thinks.

The sun is high above him, but the sky is somehow littered with thousands of shimmering stars. The moon, a silver sickle in the sky, hangs behind him as if dangled from an invisible string. At this moment, both night and day seem to be partners, surrounding Taurin with their unique lights. He looks down at the water, staring at his distorted reflection.

"My eyes," he says. "What's happened to my eyes?" Panic fills him, shaking his small frame.

"What's wrong?" A voice cries out behind him. A large hand presses against Taurin's shoulder. "Are you okay?"

"My eyes are on fire!"

Arms, thick like tree trunks, scoop Taurin up and cradle him as if he were a wounded animal. The figure holding him takes quick, heavy steps around the lake, leaving massive footprints in the loose sand. "I'll take you to Dad. He'll know what to do."

His eyes burn and his body shakes with each step forward. Taurin's thoughts twist and flip inside his head. *This isn't happening. This can't be real.* He looks up and sees who is carrying him. "Pulp?"

"We're home now," Pulp responds. His strong arms lay Taurin against a waist-high wooden table in the center of a simple kitchen. A dusty, rusted stove sits beside a stone sink that's filled to the brim with unwashed dishes. Ragged burlap fabric hangs from the corners of a rectangle window, blocking any outside light. A single bulb dangles above the table, highlighting the deep red and black grains of the wood. "Dad! Something's wrong!"

A new set of hands grip Taurin's chin, tilting his face up toward the light. "Look at me," a deep voice commands, while callused fingers pry Taurin's eyelids open. White, chalky powder slams against Taurin's exposed eyes.

"Ahhh!" Taurin cries out. "It burns!"

"Quiet," the voice responds. "It will only hurt for a second."

A white fog covers his vision, but then, as promised, the pain fades. Taurin opens and closes his eyes over and over again. Each time he does, his surroundings becoming clearer. Standing above him is his father, with brown hair cut short against his narrow head. His bushy eyebrows and dense, graying beard hide his gaunt face. Dark, colorless eyes stare down at Taurin.

"Feel better?" he asks.

"Yeah, I think so," Taurin says.

"Get up then."

Taurin sits up on the table. White powder falls from his face like fresh snow, covering the ground around him.

"What a mess," his father says.

Pulp rushes over to the corner of the room to fetch a broom, made from a crooked tree branch and a handful of yellow straw tied to one end, that's resting next to the stove. "It's no problem. I'll help clean up."

"Not the powder, you dolt!" his father scolds, curling his hands into fists.

Pulp's large frame droops like a wilted flower, his head hanging low. "Then what?"

"Look at him!" his father yells. Taurin's dad stares at his brother with cold, cruel eyes, and he presses a single finger, its skin hanging loose on the bone, against Taurin's forehead.

"You killed my wife, and you won't be happy until you've killed us too!" he tells his son.

"No!" yells Taurin. "I didn't mean to hurt anybody!"

A shock of bright light jolts him, knocking him from the table. A calm, familiar female voice crackles in his ear like static. "Taurin," she says. "Can you hear me?"

"What?" Taurin asks, his mind still disorientated from the fall. The small kitchen has been replaced with darkness, and although his eyes are open and searching, he sees nothing. "What happened?"

"I'm sorry to interrupt this way again, but I must speak with you."

"Echo?"

"Yes," she says, her voice scratchy and tense.

"I can barely hear you."

"It's growing more difficult to find a way to make contact with you. Everything here is strained."

"Is Pulp all right?"

"Yes, but not for long. You must find a way to get here soon. Please, hurry."

"I'm on my way right now! Can you just let me talk with my brother for a minute? I need to be sure he's okay."

"I'm sorry, I ..."

A loud screech screams in Taurin's ears, then there's silence. "Echo?" he yells. "Echo, answer me! Are you there?"

Suddenly the darkness is gone, and the vibrant colors of the forest flood his vision. The night, with all its terrors, has passed, and a new morning has arrived. His arms reach behind him, searching for Violet. Only grass and dirt rub against his hands. She's gone.

"Violet!" Taurin yells, springing to his feet. "Violet!" He sprints through the forest, his chest rising and falling with rapid breaths of hot air. Sweat pours from his face; his sandals crush patches of budding wild flowers beneath them. He swings his long arms like machetes, hacking tall ferns and saplings that stand in his way. She could be anywhere, but something keeps pulling him forward.

Then the thick hanging vines and potbellied trees separate, revealing a shimmering turquoise body of water. It's not nearly as large as the one in his dream, but the sparkling greens and blues are far more vibrant. Violet stands next to the lake whispering into a small metal object that she grips in her hand.

Her head moves side to side, swirling her dark hair in the air. *She's looking for someone*, Taurin thinks.

Taurin shrinks behind a tall, fat fern, its fanning leaves shielding him from her view. His eyes, their crimson flecks burning, lock on the object in Violet's hand. Half the length of her hand, and just as wide, the silver-plated device is something he's never seen before. Clear buttons cover one side and faint audio crackles out the back.

"I can't talk now," Violet whispers. She presses a clear button, reattaches the object to a thin metal chain around her neck, and stuffs it beneath her shirt. Her nervous eyes scan the area before she starts moving toward the clearing.

Taurin scoots back, pressing hard against the rugged bark of the tree. His hearts sinks low in his chest. The one person he was sure he could trust is hiding something, but why?

"Taurin?" Violet asks, blocking the sun with her hand. "Is that you?"

Taurin steps out from behind his cover and moves toward the girl. "Violet!" he yells. "I've been looking everywhere for you."

"I got turned around," she answers. "This forest all looks the same, and I couldn't find my way back to you." She curls her arm around Taurin's waist, squeezing him. "I knew you'd find me if I stayed by this lake."

Her arms feel good pressed against him, comforting. The fresh wild flowers in her hair above her right ear smell sweet, and for a moment, Taurin wants to forget about the silver object hung around her neck.

"What's the matter?" Violet asks, releasing her arms.

You're hiding something from me! Taurin wants to yell, but instead he stands silent. Pulp's life is in danger, and that's the only thing that matters. "I had another dream."

"Echo?"

"Yeah," he says, rubbing his forehead with his fingers. "Pulp doesn't have much time."

"Then we're going to need this," Violet says. She steps back and pulls a collection of bent branches and piled leaves away, revealing a sparkling ash speeder.

Taurin's eyes, drunk with wonder, examine each bolt and seam along the gray metal frame. A brown, hand-stitched leather seat sits low against a fire-red fuel tank. The speeder's two rubber tires, their tread not even worn, are shielded by a pair of silver wheel covers. "I've never seen one this nice," Taurin says, turning his stare to Violet. "Where did you get it?"

"I found it," Violet says, looking away. "Someone must have forgotten where they stashed it."

"What's this?" Taurin asks, pointing to three black markings on the fuel tank. "It looks like some kind of brand."

"No idea," replies Violet, "looks like claw marks."

Taurin leaps onto the back of the speeder, the front and rear shocks bouncing with his weight. "Hop on," he says, his arm stretching toward the girl. "Morning is already fading. If we are going to make it to the Wasteland by nightfall, we need to hurry."
"You don't need to ask me twice!" she says, tossing her legs over the rear of the speeder.

With a turn of the key and a twist of the throttle, the ash-colored machine roars to life. "Hold on!" Taurin yells over the rumble of the engine. "It's time we find Shrift!"

CHAPTER 7: WASTELAND

DUST spills over the worn racing goggles Taurin found dangling on the speeder's handlebars. The goggles' round lenses, made from smooth glass, sit snug in their copper frame; a black leather strap locks them tight against his wavy brown hair. His eyes, splashed with crimson, are protected from the elements, but his mind, still exposed to hazards of his thoughts, is vulnerable. *Save Pulp. Trust no one.*

Sleep, though interrupted by the countless pits and bumps of the crooked roadway, comforts Violet. She spent the previous night pushing through the tangles of the forest, searching for a place to send a message. Now that it's been delivered, she lets the low growl of the speeder's engine put her in a trance. Her fingers, woven together like the thin, wooden strips of a basket, lock tight around Taurin's chest.

Paths once covered with ferns and wildflowers have been swallowed by scorched sand and lines of gray, jagged mountains. Onyx-colored trees, their branches twisted and leafless, spot the otherwise barren landscape. Even the hot, dry air smells dangerous. The Wasteland is where everything goes to die.

Finally, Taurin quiets the engine. The rubber tires stop rolling, and he pulls the copper goggles off his face. His father took his brother and him many places when they were younger, before the crimson flecks had changed everything, but he had never brought them here. He'd told stories about the sand and the mountains that filled this part of Cinder, yet each time he finished the stories with, "It's not a good place to find yourself."

"Too late," Taurin mutters.

"What's that?" Violet asks, her arms stretching high above her head. She allows a loud yawn to escape her stretched mouth.

"We're here."

"That was fast," she says, sliding off the rear of the speeder. Her hand-braided straw sandals press against the sizzling sand. Her legs, which are not used to standing, wobble a little before locking tightly under her. "This is the Wasteland?"

"Looks like it," Taurin replies, still sitting on the leather seat.

"It's just so …" she turns in a circle, her eyes looking over the entire area.

"Just so what?" Taurin asks.

"Empty."

Taurin doesn't reply; he climbs off the speeder and rubs his lower back with his hands. The drive was long and the roads were rough and often uncleared; Taurin had to be alert and ready for anything. Now the Wasteland stares him in the face. Its dark mountains, stretching to the sky like broken shards of gray glass, warn the boy to stay away. He can't listen. Somewhere in this land of sand and sun is the only hope of saving his brother. *Shrift*.

"Looks like we'll have to walk," Violet says, motioning to the endless miles of harsh landscape that stretch out in front of her.

"Yeah, she'll never make it through that stuff," Taurin says, patting the side of the ash speeder. "Help me roll her behind those rocks over there." He points to a collection of red and gray stones piled in a half circle around the base of a colossal black boulder.

"I didn't realize the speeder was a girl," Violet says, gripping the rear of the machine, a soft smile curling her lips. "Does *she* have a name?"

"Ruby."

"I like that. It fits her."

"I thought so," Taurin says, rolling the speeder toward the boulder. "I don't like leaving her behind, but what choice do we have?"

"Ruby will be fine." Violet releases the speeder, leaning it against the rocks. "I'm more worried about us."

She's right, Taurin thinks. His eyes drink in the darkening landscape: mountains, canyons, and acres of sand. There's no water and no sign of an easy meal, just the emptiness of a never-ending scene of death. Black scavenger birds, their wings outstretched, circle above, waiting. "Let's just keep moving. Maybe we'll get lucky and find a place to rest."

"I'm starving," Violet says, her words sharp. "My stomach hurts, and my head is throbbing."

"In case you haven't noticed, we're in the middle of nowhere. Am I supposed to summon food from thin air like a magic trick?" Taurin leans against the boulder, his arms crossed. "Sorry to disappoint you, but it doesn't work like that."

"So touchy!" Violet says, stretching her arm toward him. "Just hand me your pack."

Taurin pulls the cracked leather straps off his shoulders and hands the backpack to her. "Take it. There's nothing in there but a bunch of junk your dad gave us."

"It's not junk," Violet says, digging through the pack. "I mean, most of it isn't." She pulls her arm from the bag with a spiraled twist of silver wire resting in the palm of her hand. "Any idea what this is?"

"A useless wire?"

"You're so helpful." Violet tosses the wire back into the bag and continues to sift through its contents. "Yes! I knew he'd know what to pack."

"What?" Taurin asks, leaning close to her. "Did you find some bread or something?"

"Better!" She pulls a glass jar capped with a yellow lid out of the pack. Small and round like a ripe apple, the jar is filled to the top with a brown substance. Violet's fingertips spin the cap clockwise, opening the jar and letting the sweet smell of wild berries fill the air.

"That smells amazing," Taurin says, his mouth watering. "What is it?"

"Berry butter!" Violet's nostrils open wide and breathe in both the tart fruit and nutty aroma of the jar's contents. "It's my dad's special recipe." Digging deep into the bag once more, Violet pulls out a pair of carved wooden spoons. "Take this," she says, handing him one of the utensils.

"Do I just dig in?"

"It's packed full of fruits and nuts, so we don't need a lot of it. Maybe just start with a spoonful."

Taurin jams his spoon deep into the brown goo, his stomach now rumbling. His tongue traces his dry lips, preparing for the rare sweetness. When the spoonful touches his tastebuds, orange and blue fireworks explode in his mind as the butter's flavors, both bitter and savory, dance in his mouth. "Amazing," he mumbles.

Violet, her bright white teeth showing between her red lips, licks her buttered spoon clean. "I told you." She rests her head against Taurin's neck; her river of hair spills over his shoulder like a waterfall. "You need to learn to trust me."

Silence falls over the pair, leaving only the rustle of the wind to respond to Violet's words. Taurin, his heart wanting to trust but his mind knowing better, sits quiet. The jam feels good in his stomach. Violet had found the speeder and provided food for the night, but that doesn't change anything.

A low, violent rumble shakes the area. Rocks rattle free from the surrounding mountains, slamming against the ground. Swirls of sand spin wildly in the distance. Something is moving.

"What is that?" Violet yells, leaping to her feet. "It feels like something is coming this way!"

Taurin's face turns pale. Cold beads of sweat roll down the back of his neck. His father's stories of the wild beasts and untamed monsters that fill the Wasteland fog his mind with fear.

"The Wasteland is an easy place to die," his father had once said. "Nothing there wants anything else to live."

"Taurin!" Violet says, shrieking. "What is that?"

A creature, its head larger than the black boulder the speeder now rests behind, stands a few hundred feet in the distance. Its round black eyes, each the size of Taurin's head, sit above a single, twisted tusk that pierces through the brown fur covering the beast's face. A row of bones line its back like a mountain range of sharpened spears. Spit pours from its mouth, which is filled with crooked, yellow teeth, all sharp enough to chew through stone.

"I don't know," Taurin says, his mouth moving, but his body frozen. "But don't move."

"That's your plan?" Violet whispers.

"Have a better one?"

"Flames!" she says, much louder than she expected.

The beast's head snaps toward her. Its green eyes burn through her with a fervent gaze that makes her whole body shiver. The creature's hot breath spills out of its unhinged mouth like a dark mist, smelling like rotten fruit and spoiled meat. Violet places her hand over her nose, the smell causing her to gag. "Burn that thing!" she yells.

Heat flushes Taurin's eyes as his mind focuses solely on an image of a red, crackling flame. The ground shakes under his feet, causing him to lose his balance and his train of thought for a moment. The beast rushes toward him, its four massive paws smashing against the sand. *Focus. Stay calm.*

"BURN!" Taurin yells, the word ripping from his throat. Flames pour from his fingertips, lighting the night sky with vibrant oranges and reds. The heat is so intense, it knocks Violet from her feet. Her body slams against the ground, but Taurin can't stop to check on her. The searing fire leaping from his fingers is the only thing keeping the beast from making them its dinner.

The creature lets out a wild roar, the sound rattling the area like an earthquake as Taurin's blaze scorches the ground in front of it. The fire burns white-hot. Even with its massive size and sharpened row of horns running down its back, the creature doesn't dare test these flames.

"We need to get out of here!" Violet shouts, her voice rising over the beast's cries. "Help me up." Her outstretched hand, fingers spread wide, reaches for Taurin.

Smoke crawls toward the twinkling stars, the flames growing taller by the second, but fire no longer spits from Taurin's fingers. Instead, they wrap themselves tightly around Violet's slender wrist. One strong yank pulls her off the ground. "Let's move," he says.

They run hand in hand, the auburn blaze behind them and the black night in front of them. The creature growls, rattling the rocks and dust beneath their sandals as it battles the flames. Taurin looks back, his crimson flecks still burning brightly in his eyes, and sees something that makes his stomach sour. With its legs bent back and its claws dug deeply into the sand, the creature leaps forward, clearing the wall of fire.

"It's coming!" Taurin yells.

"I thought you'd roasted that thing," Violet shouts, "but you just made it mad!"

Sprinting, Taurin leaps over a mound of loose sand, then slides against a fallen slab of stone. His right shoulder scrapes against the jagged edge of the tumbled rock, ripping his shirt and tearing a deep gash in his flesh. Taurin grimaces and grabs at his wound with his filth-covered fingers. "It's not that easy!"

"Apparently not!" Violet says.

"Next time, you can let fire rip through your body and see how it turns out!" Taurin shakes his head. The wild animal's twisted tusk could soon rip through his flesh like a wet paper bag, and all he can think about is how his powers didn't impress Violet. *Focus*, he tells himself.

The beast, which is obviously riled with anger, closes in on the pair. Its hot breath splatters the sand with thick globs of spit and slime. The creature's thick, purple tongue smacks against its dark lips as it chases them.

"Look!" Violet says, gesturing toward a jagged opening at the base of a nearby mountain. Just a few inches wider than the girl's body and half as tall, the cave would be a tight squeeze for her and almost impossible for Taurin to fit.

"You'll have to run for it," Taurin says, his chest burning from the relentless pace almost as much as the gash in his shoulder. "I'll cause a distraction."

"That thing will kill you!"

A thunderous growl echoes off the mountains, muting Violet's warning. Taurin lets go of Violet's hand and turns to face the beast. Its green eyes stand out against the night sky like two glowing orbs. The creature's yellowed teeth, wet with saliva, reflect the moon's pale light.

Taurin stretches his arms wide, and curls his fingers into fists. His own eyes, narrowed and focused, burn with red fire. *"Come and get me!"*

CHAPTER 8: SHRIFT

THE CREATURE'S four massive paws, covered with matted brown fur, slam against the Wasteland's shifting sand. Slime and spit drip from its flapping purple tongue; fury fills its green eyes.

Taurin stands rigid, his fingers curled into fists and his eyes red with fire. The hot wind whips around his body. Grains of sand attack his face like angry bees, stinging his cheeks. Violet is hidden behind him, now protected in the cave. The beast stands in front of him, coming closer by the second. *Be brave*, he tells himself.

Fear, an aching terror, burrows deep into his bones. It's a fright so powerful it hurts. Even with all his powers, Taurin is still only a boy. His years haven't prepared him to be in this moment—to be in charge of their fates. He should be *protected* by someone, not protecting. Moments don't care about readiness, he realizes. They just happen.

Another roar rumbles and shakes Taurin's core, rattling his bones. Warm, rancid breath pushes through the air, filling his nose. The smell knocks him back a step, melting him from his stance. Taurin's fists uncurl. His eyes empty of crimson. He is no longer ready to face the wild beast; his powers, his nerves have failed him.

"Move!" a coarse voice shouts. Then, like a hammer striking a nail, a wide shoulder as solid as stone crashes against his body, flattening him on the sand. "Stay down."

Taurin rubs loose grains of sand and dust from his eyes. His vision blurs, and his thoughts tangle. *What is happening?*

A stranger, his face concealed by a ripped khaki scarf, now stands between Taurin and the beast. The stranger wears tall leather boots that cover his feet and thick calves, stopping just under his knees. A metal helmet, its green paint chipped away from age, sits crooked atop the man's head. Goggles conceal his eyes, and a dark tint coats the glass. The stranger's long, burlap coat is ripped and patched with mismatched pieces of cloth, but it covers his broad frame. His hands, covered with brown leather gloves, grip a sharpened tree branch.

Taurin looks up. The man stands above him, his spear pointed toward the beast. "That's not going to stop him!" he yells, his heart slamming against the bones of his chest. The stranger looks down at him, and even though the tattered scarf hides the lower half of his face, Taurin can tell that the stranger is smiling.

The man presses a single finger against his lips. "Shhhh," he whispers. Then he turns and hurls the makeshift spear toward the growling beast. The branch, which is not quite straight but also not crooked, soars through the air like a rocket. Its gray bark twists like a tornado. The beast lets loose a final ground-shaking roar before the tip of the wooden spear finds its neck.

Like a sharp knife through melting butter, the branch slices the beast's throat and a river of crimson spills from the wound and mixes with the brown sand. Its fierce green eyes turn black. The creature's purple tongue, still dripping with slime, hangs limp as its body slumps to the ground. The massive beast lies dead just inches from Taurin's face.

The stranger reaches toward Taurin with a gloved hand. "Take it," he commands, his voice gruff and stern.

"Take what?" Taurin asks, confused. Moments before, with his fists clenched and fire in his eyes, he was staring at the snarling monster. But instead of facing the beast, something else happened. *Someone else.*

With a strong, almost painful grip, the stranger reaches down and takes a hold of Taurin's arm, pulling him from the ground. Taurin shakes his head, like a dog does after a bath, sending dust and sand flying in every direction. Loud, dry coughs rake his throat.

"Here," the man says, tossing a metal canteen at Taurin's feet. "Drink."

He quickly twists the container's cap open and takes rapid gulps, soothing his dry throat. The water, though metallic and warm, tastes wonderful to Taurin. He rubs the back of his hand across his cracked lips, wiping away any remaining moisture.

For a moment everything feels perfect: the beast is dead, Violet is safe, and his throat is wet. The feeling doesn't last. The buzz of a charging heat pistol reminds Taurin that he's not alone.

"Give it up," the man says through his scarf. The pistol, made from an intricate combination of copper and wood, is pointed at Taurin's chest.

Beads of sweat drip down Taurin's forehead. His throat, though recently wet from his drink, goes dry again. "What do you want?" he asks, his words raspy and quiet.

"Water," the man says. "Toss it over." The copper pistol's steam engine hums in the man's hand; its barrel now pointed at

Taurin's head. One blast from this beautiful, deadly weapon would end everything.

"Here," Taurin says. "I don't want any trouble." He throws the canteen to the ground. The metal container lands with a thud in front of the man's leather boots. *Glug. Glug. Glug.* Taurin looks down and nearly forgets to breathe. For a moment, it even feels as though his heart stops beating. Water pours from the canteen, melting into the dry ground. Taurin still holds the round cap in his right hand. In his rush, he'd forgotten to twist it back on. *Stupid.*

The man falls to his knees and scoops up the canteen, dropping the pistol in the process. "No! No! No!" he shouts. "You've killed me!"

In a flash, Taurin dives to the ground. Plumes of sand float to the sky, blinding the area for a moment. He frantically searches for the pistol until his fingers brush against cool metal. He slowly picks up the weapon and wraps his index finger around the heat pistol's sickled trigger. He stands with his arm outstretched, the pistol aimed to kill. "Get up," he says.

"Go ahead," the stranger says. "Shoot." His index finger points directly at the center of Taurin's forehead. "Pull the trigger."

"Get up!" Taurin says again, now shouting. "I'll do it!"

"I'm dead already." The man drops flat against the sand. His arms spread out beside him. "Get it done with."

Taurin rests his finger against the trigger and swallows hard. This man had both saved his life and tried to take it all in the span of a few minutes. He shakes his head. The Wasteland is already proving to be a place he doesn't want to be.

A familiar hand presses against Taurin's shoulder, startling him. "He saved our lives," Violet says.

"Great," the man says, spitting his words. "A girl."

Violet walks over to him and offers her hand. "No one is going to die tonight."

"Comforting," he says as he smacks Violet's hand away. He stands and knocks dust from his coat and pants. A moment passes, then he turns to Taurin. "Hand it over."

"No way," Taurin says, keeping the pistol aimed at the stranger. "You were going to kill me."

"If I wanted to kill you, you'd be killed. Now quit trying to impress your girl and give it over." The man takes a step toward Taurin. "You a thief?"

"You dropped it! I'm just protecting myself."

The man takes another step, his masked face now just inches away from Taurin. "You…a…thief?"

"I'm not!"

"Then give it!" He smacks at the pistol with his gloved hand, knocking it away from Taurin. But just before the wooden grip hits the ground, the gun stops falling.

"Get back here," the man commands. As if it had heard the order, the copper gun flies back into his palm. He says nothing; just nods, holsters the weapon, and turns to walk away.

"How did you do that?" Violet asks, her eyes wide with wonder. "I mean—"

"None of your business how," he interrupts. "Just know I can, and that's enough." He kneels down in front of the fallen beast and pulls a concealed knife from his right boot. Its razor-sharp, curved blade has a handle wrapped with torn brown cloth and strips of black leather. The knife, just longer than six inches, looks fierce in his hand.

"Like Taurin said, we don't want trouble."

"What you want isn't my concern." The stranger slices the blade through the beast's flesh, cutting through the thick brown fur with ease. In seconds, the tusk lays on the sand, blood coloring its roots. The man ties the bone to a rope that he pulls from his coat pocket and tosses it over his shoulder; the tip drags behind him in the sand.

"You owe us an explanation," Taurin says.

The stranger turns, his steps slow, and walks toward Taurin. One hand slides the bloodied knife back into his boot; the other unwraps the scarf around his face and then pulls off his goggles. Brown stubble, coated with dust and filth, covers his chin. His blue eyes, which are littered with flecks of white, cast their intense glare on Taurin. "I don't owe nobody nothing. Especially you."

"Organic," Violet says, raising her hands and pressing them against her cheeks. "You're—"

"I'm no one!" He shouts.

"You're like me," Taurin points first to his own eyes, then to the man's. "Marked."

A glob of spit flies from the stranger's mouth and splatters in front of Taurin's sandals. "I'm not."

The moon, bright and full, shines a pale light on the man, revealing a face much younger than Taurin had expected. The stranger's worn clothes and skill with the spear and blade had led him to believe this person was older—a grown man. Now, unmasked and illuminated, Taurin sees that this is the face of someone just a little older than he is. "You're young," Taurin says.

"Older than you. What are you, twelve?"

"Fifteen!"

"You look twelve."

"You look like …"

"I look like what I am—a crook, a killer, and an all-around bad guy. It would be in your best interest to let me be." He steps toward Taurin. "Understand?"

"Oh, you don't look so bad to me," Violet says, her words more song than statement. "You seem like a guy who can get things done."

"Oh yeah?"

"Yeah." Violet walks over and brushes her fingers against his shoulder. "What did you say your name was again?"

"I didn't."

"Shame," Violet says, turning her back to him. "We're looking for a man with special skills, but that's clearly not you." She looks at Taurin and winks—a silent signal the pair have used since childhood. *Play along.*

"Let's just get out of here," Taurin says to Violet, catching her clue. "He's probably too stupid to know what to do with the reward."

In a flash, the stranger pulls the curved blade, still dripping with blood, from his boot again and presses it against Taurin's throat. "Call me stupid again. I dare you."

"We are just looking for someone," Violet says. "Just put the knife down and we'll leave."

"Sorry," Taurin croaks, the blade still pushing against his throat. "I didn't realize you were so sensitive."

"Sorry ain't enough. I want that reward."

A small, confident smile curls Violet's lips. "We're looking for someone."

"And who's that?"

"Put the knife down and I'll tell you," Violet says.

"Nah, I'd rather cut his throat."

"Shrift," Taurin murmurs. "We're looking for someone called Shrift."

"Would this *Shrift* get your reward?"

"Yes," Violet answers. "Do you know him?"

The stranger looks at Violet, his blue eyes sparkling in the faint moonlight.

"Honey, I am him."

SHRIFT

CHAPTER 9: NEEDS & WANTS

THE SHARP tip of Shrift's knife, still damp with crimson, picks at his front teeth. A rusted metal can, filled with a mix of black beans and shredded greens, sits next to a small fire. Dry twigs and grasses pop and hiss while the modest meal cooks. Shrift doesn't look behind him to see what his new companions are up to.

"What's he doing?" Taurin whispers to Violet. "He's been poking that can for an hour."

Violet shrugs. "Just leave him alone."

"Why should I?"

"Because we need him, and whatever he's cooking actually smells pretty good."

Taurin breathes in the burnt smells wafting through the night air. Saliva gathers on his tongue, and his stomach rumbles with hunger. "Got to be better than that berry stuff your dad gave us.

Violet crosses her arms and looks away. "That *stuff* probably kept us alive."

"I know, I was just—"

"Just what?" Violet interrupts, her words hot. "Just being thankless to someone who actually cares if we survive out here? *Just* being so shallow that you'll complain about the one thing that's kept us alive? Just …"

The clang of metal hitting metal rings out in the night. "If you two crows are done crying at each other long enough to eat something, the beans are done. If not, that's just more for me," Shrift says.

"Oh, we're done." Violet shoots Taurin a final glare and walks over to the fire.

"Look I didn't mean …"

"Don't matter what you meant, does it?" Shrift says, taking a step toward Taurin. "She's just tired of you is all."

Taurin's cheeks flush bright red. "What do you know? You're nobody!"

"Oh I'm a little more than that." Shrift's blue eyes blur to a milky white. His thick fingers curl into fists the size of coconuts. "Some might say I'm special." Silver scales, each overlapping the next, crawl up his brawny arms until his entire body is covered, save for his eyes.

Taurin takes a step back. The sight of the silver creature in front of him takes a moment to process. Shrift's body, though always thick, now ripples with piles of bulging muscles. Canvas clothes that had hung loose on him earlier now suck tight to his widened body. "What are you?" he asks.

Shrift lets loose a heavy laugh, his voice booming like a bass drum. "Guess you are as dumb as you look."

Taurin's temper flares. He widens his stance, lowers his shoulders, and stretches his hands out in front of his body. "If you want me, come get me!"

Each of Shrift's steps shakes the sand beneath Taurin's feet. His silver scales shift like chainmail on his body. "You'll regret finding me, kid," he says just before he pulls back his massive right fist and crashes it against Taurin's chest.

The impact sucks the air from Taurin's lungs and rattles his brain. Circles of stars fly through his mind. The blow, the fiercest he's ever felt, sends him crashing to the ground. He can't seem to keep his eyes open, and sleep calls to him. The sound of booming laughter, however, shakes Taurin from his daze. Shrift, his scales still covering his body, towers above him, laughing.

"This is pathetic," Shrift says. "One hit and you crumple like a wet sack of sand?"

"Just leave him alone!" Violet yells. "You're going to hurt him!"

"Honey, I plan on doing more than that." Shrift turns toward Taurin once again, fixing his white-hot eyes on the boy. "Your lady wants me to take it easy on you. What do you say?"

Taurin fills his lungs with long gulps of hot air. The circling stars in his mind scatter into the skies above him, brightening his vision. His eyes burn wild with flecks of crimson. A power stirs inside him unlike any he's felt before. Fear grips him, but not fear of the enemy above him—fear of the power inside of him.

"Make your choice already!" Shrift demands. "Die crying or die fighting?"

"You were supposed to help us!" Violet pleads.

Shrift turns to her, his face hard. "Get used to disappointment."

"Leave her out of this!" Taurin yells, leaping up from the ground and clasping his hands around Shrift's scaled neck. Not flames or fire, but rather pure energy explodes from the tips of his fingers, sending waves through Shrift's body and bringing the silver giant to his knees.

"Is that the best you got?" Shrift coughs, spitting a stream of blood on Taurin's sandals. "It hurts more when I shave."

Taurin squeezes his hands tighter, and like a river of smoldering lava, streams of red light begin to crack through Shrift's skin. Scales that were once as hard as stone now fall to the ground like chunks of dry tree bark. Blood drips from Shrift's body like rain from a cloud. "Is this what you wanted?" Taurin asks, his body shaking. "Does this prove anything?"

As quick as the scales appeared, they vanish, leaving just the rough skin of Shrift's neck between Taurin's clenched hands. A strange smile covers Shrift's face, revealing a line of white teeth splattered with red. His blue eyes, now soft and flecked with white, stare at Taurin with a look that can only be described as happiness. "It's true, then," Shrift croaks, his throat still constricted. "You're him."

Taurin lets go of his foe's neck and takes a few steps back, startled by Shrift's words. He looks down to his hands, which were once pulsing with power but are now calm. The same kind of bones that make up other people's hands are wrapped in his tan skin, yet something flows beneath the surface that's unique. He's known that he was different since he was young. Now, with every wild burst of energy, it becomes clear that *different* doesn't quite describe it. "Who am I?" Taurin asks, his eyes still studying his fingers.

Shrift's long fingers wipe fresh blood and sand away from his cracked lips, and he spits a mouthful of colored liquid on the ground. "You're the one they're looking for."

The image of a man with pleated pants tucked into tall black boots, a flashlight in one hand and a heat pistol gripped tightly in the other, and a red *WF* stitched onto a tailored suit jacket flashes in Taurin's mind. "Watch Force," Taurin mumbles.

"Yup, and they've been hunting you for a while."

"How do you know that?" Violet asks before removing a rag from Taurin's pack, dampening it with medicine, and placing it on Shrift's bloody lip.

"Youch!" Shrift cries out, pulling the cloth from his mouth. "What the heck is on that?"

"Quit being such a baby and hold it still," she says.

"What is it?"

"Just a cream my dad made. It stings but does the trick, so put it back."

"Honey, I'm going to need more than a little cream." Shrift pulls his coat off first, then his shirt. Strips of flesh hang like ribbons from his toned chest and tight stomach from where his scales fell off during the fight with Taurin. Violet slaps her hand over her mouth, trying hard not to wretch at the sight. "That bad, huh?"

"I'm sorry," Violet says. "I just wasn't expecting that." She dips her fingers into a container of white cream and moves toward Shrift. "This is going to hurt."

Shrift waves his arm, motioning for Violet to put the cream back. "No need for that stuff. Just come here." He reaches out and grabs a hold of Violet's arm. "Just take a minute."

Frozen, Violet looks into Shrift's cool blue eyes. She watches as the small flecks grow into an ocean of white, blocking out all other color in his eyes. Then there's heat. Warmth trickles up her arm, causing the fine hairs on her arms to bristle. She looks down at Shrift's stomach, and to her amazement, sees the flaps of ripped skin pull tightly against his body until not a single scratch remains. "Amazing."

"I'm a man of many talents," Shrift says, a cocky smile on his face. "Though I couldn't have done it without you." He places his hand on Violet's. "You healed me."

Violet rips her hand out from under his. "I didn't, and I don't like being played." She glances at Taurin to catch his response. He's distracted, rubbing cream on the wound the beast left him with earlier

"Touchy." Shrift says, smiling. He pulls his blood-stained shirt on over his head.

"Seriously, how'd you do that?" she asks.

"I think you know."

Violet rolls her eyes and walks over to sit by the fire. The can of stew sits just outside of the flames. She reaches down, picks it up, and breathes in the harsh smells of burnt leaves and roasted beans. "Would be a better trick if you could actually cook."

"Oh, it's not that bad," Shrift says, sitting down close to her. "Let me have a smell." He buries his nose deep into the can and sucks in a long breath. Then, like a jack in the box, he snaps his head back at shouts, "Oh, Mama, that's the good stuff!"

Violet giggles loudly. It's not a laugh that's forced or fake, but rather a pure howl that shakes every part of her body. She wipes tears from her eyes and slams a fist against Shrift's arm. "You scared me!" She smiles again before scooping a handful of stew from the can in Shrift's hand and swallowing the food. So much seriousness and worry forgotten in a moment. For a moment.

"Sorry to interrupt your little party," Taurin says, his voice hard. "You said someone is hunting me."

Startled, Shrift and Violet turn to see him standing behind them. With his arms crossed at his chest and his eyes narrowed, he looks more like an angry parent than a peer.

"Almost forgot you were here," Shrift says, turning back to the fire. "But there you are."

"Yes, here I am!" Taurin snaps. "And I am done with all your stupid games and your cryptic sayings!"

"Calm down, Taurin; I'm sure he has a reason for all of this," Violet says, glancing at Shrift.

Taurin shakes his head in disgust. "So, you're taking his side now?"

Violet stands. "No, I'm not taking anyone's side. You're just acting like a jerk!"

"He tries to kill us. I saved our lives, and somehow I'm the jerk in all of this?" Taurin slams his palms against the side of his head. "I just want this all to be over."

"Keep wishin' because it's not close to over." Shrift pushes two fingers deep into the can and pulls out a thick helping of the stew, then shoves the mix into his mouth. "Mmm…that's good," he mumbles around his fingers.

"Useless," Taurin scoffs. "You're just a reject, like me."

"That's true, so just sit down and have some." Shrift offers the can to Taurin and pats the sand beside him. "I swear, I won't bite."

The grumble in his stomach outweighs his anger, and Taurin gives in and takes the can. One handful of the stew fills his mouth, then his belly. "It's pretty terrible," Taurin says, sitting down in front of the fire. "Offense intended."

"None taken," Shrift replies.

The distinct sounds of heaving and wretching startle him. He sees Violet, bent over and holding her stomach, vomiting. Taurin stands and rushes to her. "Are you okay? What happened?"

"She's fine," Shrift says. "Just the beans working their magic." He pushes another handful of the hot stew into his mouth. "You're next."

Violet wipes her mouth off with the back of her hand. "What did you put in that stuff?"

"Don't worry about that. Worry about what's inside you that's making you puke your guts out."

The only word Taurin can get out is, "What?" before he too spills his stomach's contents all over the ground.

Still licking the creamy stew off his fingers, Shrift stands, cocks his head to one side, and walks over to Violet. "Seems to me you're hidin' something. Time to find out what."

CHAPTER 10: VIOLET'S TRUTH

CHEEK'S BURNING red-hot and her eyes wet with tears, Violet stares down at the contents of her stomach now lying in a puddle of thick liquid on the ground. The tears are not from pain, but rather, from shame. She knew this moment had to come, of course, but she didn't expect it to arrive so soon. Like most people with secrets, she thought that she'd pick the time to reveal them. The truth, however, always has a way of revealing itself. *Shrift*.

"How ya feeling there, darling?" Shrift asks, kneeling down next to Violet. "Sorry to make you spill your guts in front of your boyfriend, but it had to be done. I'm sure you understand." He stands and brushes the dirt off his pants.

"Why did you do this to us?" Taurin, who is now finished heaving, asks. "I thought—"

"You need to stop thinking so much and pay attention to what's going on around you," Shrift says, his words hard. "This girl of yours is hiding something, and you haven't got a clue. What kind of idiot goes looking for some stranger in the desert without asking more questions about why first?"

"You don't know anything," Taurin spits. "My brother—"

"Yeah, yeah," Shrift interrupts again. "I know all about your brother and his *situation*."

Taurin glares at his new companion. "If you know something, you need to tell me!"

"Just cool your heels for a minute. First things' first." Shrift bends over and sticks his finger into the warm liquid pooling in front of Violet. Like a dog sniffing his food, he breathes in the rank, metallic scent of the bile. He focuses his eyes on the yellow fluid for a few stretched seconds. "That sure is a strange liquid. Recognize it?" His question is for Violet, though Taurin speaks first.

"It's puke. What's so interesting about that?"

"Nothing, I suppose. Unless she thinks it might be something more." Shrift's eyes narrow into a thin squint. "Have anything to add?" He looks pointedly at Violet.

Conflicting voices rattle inside Violet's skull. *Say something. Keep quiet.* Tell the truth. *He'll never forgive you.*

He should know why. Just lie. "I had to do it," Violet mutters. "It wasn't my choice."

Taurin, his eyes dazed, looks over to Violet. "Had to do what?" he asks. "Violet, what's going on?"

"Yeah, what's going on?" Shrift chirps. "Have you been bad?"

"Just shut up already," Violet says, walking a few steps away. "I don't owe you anything. I just want Taurin to know the truth."

"Oh, that's very brave of you and all, but you seem to forget you do need my help. So, whatever you've worked up the courage to tell your boy over there"—he points at Taurin—"you can tell me."

Violet brushes long strands of her raven hair back with trembling fingers, hooking them behind her ears. "Fine, you seem to know everything already, so why don't you tell him?"

"I just know the *what*, not the *why*. So, you'll have to fill in the details for me. Wait a sec though. I need to grab something." Shrift digs deep into a pocket on the inside of his coat and pulls out a clear bag filled with roasted desert beetles. "You can go ahead now. I just wanted a snack for the show." He sits on the sand, crosses his legs, and tosses a handful of the crispy bugs into his mouth, crunching them loudly. His eyes, filled with a juvenile excitement, lock on Violet. "Go on, get to the good part!"

A sheen of sweat covers Violet's forehead. Normally the sight of someone swallowing a mouthful of beetles, cooked or otherwise, would have made her sick, but her mind is too distracted to care. "Taurin," she says after a few moments. "I haven't been completely truthful with you."

Taurin says nothing, his arms crossed, stance rigid. His cold eyes, however, reveal his thoughts. *I trusted you.*

"I lied, but I had to," Violet continues, her voice growing louder by the second. "You were so fixed on your brother, and your dad had just been killed, so I just didn't think you could handle anything else."

"This is good stuff," Shrift chimes in, still munching on the beetles. "Get on with it!"

"Let me finish!" Violet shouts. "Just eat your disgusting bugs and keep your mouth shut." Shrift makes a zipping motion over his lips, then locks them with an imaginary key. Violet rolls her eyes. "You're a child."

"You were explaining how your lie was protecting me," Taurin says, his arms still crossed. "Care to explain?"

Violet clears her throat and moves toward her friend. "I wasn't protecting *you*," she says and then pauses, her eyes

searching the ground for the right words. "I was protecting …
someone else."

A loud, obnoxious crunching noise causes Taurin and
Violet to shoot matching glares at Shrift. "Sorry," he mouths.
Crunch. Crunch.

Taurin shakes his head and focuses on Violet again. "Does
this have to do with that thing around your neck?"

"What *thing*?"

"Your necklace. I saw you talking to it in the woods. Does
it have something to do with all of this?"

"You were spying on me?" Violet asks. She sets her fisted
hands on her hips. "I can't believe you would do that!"

"Are you kidding me?" Taurin responds. "Clearly I had
good reason not to trust you!"

Crunch. Crunch. CRUNCH.

Matching glares once more burn toward Shrift.

Violet rubs her eyes with the tips of her fingers. "You're
right, and I'm sorry. I just couldn't tell you."

"You didn't trust me?" Taurin asks, impatient.

"He just didn't want you to know about any of this."

"Who?"

Violet kicks the sand, making a drab cloud shoot out in front of her feet. "It's Clue."

The name hits Taurin like a lump of heavy clay. Clue, the mysterious man who trained him, had always been invisible, never showing his face and always keeping his identity a secret. Now, Violet says she is working with him? How is this possible? She was there with him through every odd note and strange challenge that led him to be here now, always acting like each revelation was new to her as well. *Maybe not*, he thinks. "You've known all along? Since the beginning?"

"It's not like that, Taurin."

"Then what's it like?" Taurin steps closer to Violet. His eyes, burning with crimson, look deep into hers. "Is it like when you told me to trust you?"

Violet covers her face with her hands and turns away from him. "You're not the only one who's lost someone."

Taurin's thoughts drift, as thoughts often do in times of stress, to the ones he's lost. Though he never knew her, his mother was the first. She died giving birth to him. A faded, gray photo was the only proof to Taurin that he even had a mother. The rest of who she was or even what she looked like was lost. Most of the evidence had been destroyed by his father after her death because he said the memories were too painful for him, and the rest eroded over time until nothing but the single pictured remained. It, too, is now lost; it was ruined in the fire.

Taurin's father was the second to be taken; his head had been severed from his body like a flower blossom from a stem. He, like so many people in Cinder, was calloused. Not just his hands from working the mines, but Taurin knew his soul was hardened too. One night, after a long day at the mine, his father confessed that his heart was shattered the day his wife died. He explained to his sons that he tried to teach them the skills they needed to survive, but he knew he'd never be able to give them what they truly needed. Taurin watched the grief eventually destroy his father, and always blamed himself.

Then there was Pulp. A giant of sorts, standing nearly a head above everyone in Cinder. He was Taurin's protector and older brother by three years. He was there for Taurin when no one else was—gentle enough to wipe away the tears of a young boy who longed for his mother, and strong enough to keep any danger at a distance. Until, of course, he couldn't. Taurin's protector was now the one who needed saving.

"Taurin?" Violet says, startling him back to the present.

He shakes his head, fluttering his eyelids to clear his vision, and fixes his sight on Violet. She stands before him, looking concerned. "I'm sorry. I was just thinking," he says.

"Are you okay?"

"No. Not really."

Violet reaches over and presses her palm against his face. Her touch feels soft against his windblown cheeks. So little time has passed, but still so much has changed. Every moment seems to bring a new revelation or challenge, each more difficult than the last. It's impossible for him to know what to think or feel. For the moment, this feels good. It feels right.

"I really am sorry," Violet whispers, her words no louder than a heartbeat.

Taurin nods. "Who did you lose?"

"My sister," she says, dropping her hand to her side. "Her name's Cay."

Crunch. Crunch. CRUNCH.

"Seriously, Shrift?" Taurin asks, shaking his head.

"Sorry, all this drama just makes me hungry."

"I'm glad our grief entertains you," Violet spits.

"I'm glad you're glad. Now, if you don't mind, stop interrupting." *Crunch. Crunch.*

"Just ignore him," Taurin says. "Let's just sit down by the fire and figure this out."

"Sounds good."

"Just don't sit in the puke. It's kinda everywhere."

"Thanks, Shrift," Violet says, sitting down next to Taurin. "Where do you want me to start?"

"I'm not sure," Taurin replies. "Why did we just puke up all that stuff?"

"Care to explain?" Violet asks Shrift. "You seem to know."

"Tracking fluid. Not high-tech, but it works just fine. Laced with little bits and pieces that someone can follow."

Violet nods. "Remember that stuff my dad made us drink?"

Taurin, of course, remembers the odd drink in the hidden room at Violet's house. The scene was so strange that it almost made sense. "So your dad is tracking us? Why?"

"Cay was taken, just like Pulp."

"Another secret," Taurin says. "How is it possible that I didn't know you had a sister?"

"My mother and her left when I was very little. My parents wanted to protect her because they knew she was special."

"And you never told me?

"I just couldn't," she pauses. "It's complicated."

"Now her and your mother are with Pulp?"

"No, my mother is safe now and we don't know if Cay is with Pulp or not, but it's the only chance we have." Violet picks up Taurin's hand and squeezes it tightly with her own. "You're special, and Dad knows that. He just didn't want to add another problem to your life."

"You could have told me," Taurin says. "You didn't need to hide all this and call him behind my back. I can deal."

"I know that now."

"No more secrets?"

Violet's eyes twitch as she shakes her head. "No," she lies. "Nothing else."

Taurin slides his hand from hers and places both of his palms near the fire. Heat tickles his fingers and warms his face. *Sizzle. Crack.* The flames are the soundtrack of the night. Too many words have been shared. It's time to sit, to gather strength, and to prepare for whatever is waiting. He motions for Shrift to hand him the bag that's now just half full of roasted beetles. He digs deep into the sack and tosses another handful into his mouth.

Crunch. Crunch. CRUNCH.

CHAPTER 11: WAKE UP

LIKE the coarse rind of a ripe orange, the night sky peels away and reveals the vibrant colors of morning. Black-stone mountains frame a morning sky filled with beautiful shades of pink and orange. The colors hover over the Wasteland like cotton—soft, weightless, and gentle. If the three travelers didn't know better, they would think this is a good place; they'd want to stay here for a while and soak up the morning light. But they do know better. Each would rather be anywhere but here.

"Mmm…that smells so good," Violet coos. She stretches her slender arms above her head, twisting into a spiral of flesh. "What is that, Shrift?" The smoky smells of seared meat fill her nose, and saliva wets her mouth. She traces her pink tongue across her dry, cracked lips as the crackle of fat frying rattles in her ears.

"Oh, now don't get yourself too excited," Shrift replies, staring down at his skillet. "It's going to leave you wanting, I'm afraid. Your belly will ask for more, so tell your brain right away that there isn't any. Understand?" He looks back at Violet. "We'll have a taste, and that's all."

"No arguments from me," Violet says as she rushes toward Shrift. A small fire burns under a charred skillet. She looks down, her mouth watering now more than ever, and sees six thin strips of meat sizzling in a shallow pool of clear liquid. "Can I try a bite?"

Shrift wags a calloused finger at Violet. "Patience," he says before tossing a pinch of white and black grains onto the meat. "Good enough is quick and easy, but good takes time." His stretched fingers wrap around the metal handle of the pan. "Ouch! It's hot!"

Violet jumps back, her eyes the size of saucers. "Just let go!" Violet yells. "It was in the fire!"

"Ha, ha, ha!" Shrift's laugh is big, as though it comes from the deep parts of his stomach. "I'm fine, darling. Just take a look here." His eyes motion for her to look down. Like the dark grime that covers the pan, Shrift's entire hand is now black. "Go on, touch it," he says, bringing his charred hand toward Violet. "Won't hurt a bit. I swear."

Ever curious, Violet presses her index finger against his outstretched hand. "It's not hot," she says, surprised. "Not even a little." Her finger traces Shrift's skin, and she's surprised to find it's hard like metal or stone, not soft like flesh. "How is this possible?"

"Oh, now, you need to give me a little more credit than that. Your friend over there isn't the only one who has magic in his veins," Shrift says. "I just sucked up a little of the pan into my hand, and there ya go. Can't burn what can't be burned."

"So you can become whatever you want?" Violet asks. "Just by thinking about it or something like that?"

"No, it's nothing like that," Shrift says. "I have to touch something. I need to feel what it feels before I can take a piece of it for myself." A silence hangs in the air for a few seconds. "I know it sounds strange and all, but I have to talk to it first."

"That's not strange." Violet places her hand against Shrift's back. "It's amazing." Her eyes sparkle with wonder; a small chill tickles her spine. "So you have to touch it?"

Shrift shakes his shoulders, knocking Violet's hand away. "I already said that," he says. "I ain't any different than the rest of 'em."

"The rest of who?"

"Organics. Just like your sister and whoever else you're looking for. We're all the same like that. Different abilities maybe, but we all need to touch or *talk* to something to make whatever we have inside us work."

"Taurin doesn't need to touch anything."

Shrift pulls his curved blade from his boot and stabs at a piece of meat in the pan. "That's 'cause he's different."

"What are you guys talking about?" Taurin asks, walking over to the pair. He rubs his eyes and yawns. "What's cooking?"

Violet yells, "Don't sneak up on me! I could have hurt you." She smacks at the cotton shirt covering Taurin's chest.

"You kind of just did." Taurin winces and rubs his chest with his hand.

"Good," Violet says and kneels beside the skillet. "Like I said, you shouldn't sneak up on people like that."

"Sorry, I didn't realize you were so sensitive."

"Morning, sunshine," Shrift says through a thin smile. "Hope you got some good shut-eye, 'cause you're gonna need it."

"Is that crickets or snails this time?" Taurin asks, pointing to the meat in the skillet. "I don't think I could stand another beetle."

"Beggars aren't choosers. Especially beggars who tried to kill me." Shrift points the tip of his knife, still skewering a strip of cooked meat, at Taurin. "So sit down and say thank you."

Taurin shakes his brown wavy hair back and forth, scattering dust in the air. "You tried to kill me too." He reaches out, snags the meat from the knife, and takes a bite. Sweet, smoky flavors flood his mouth, and his eyes roll back into his head. It's been years since he's had meat prepared like this; it's the way his father cooked it when Taurin was younger. His father would grill strips of wild beast, whatever type was hunted that day, over a campfire each night after one of their adventures. Those were good days for Taurin and his brother. "Not bad," he says.

"Your face says it's better than that," Violet says. "I thought you were going to pass out there for a second." She smiles, her two rows of perfect white teeth shining between her rose-colored lips. A gust of wind twists her hair, and the now-risen sun glows orange behind her. For a moment Taurin doesn't say anything. He can't take his eyes off her, because nothing has ever looked so beautiful in his entire life. Violet catches a handful of her hair and tucks it behind her ear again. "Are you all right?" she asks.

Taurin nods. "Yeah, I'm still drowsy is all." Blood rushes to his face, painting his cheeks a bright red. He turns quickly to Shrift. "This is better than the beetles."

The three companions sit together for a while, each taking small bites of their two pieces of cooked meat. The flavors are excellent, the best any have had for days. It's the amount of food that's the issue. As Shrift predicted, it's not nearly enough protein to fill their bellies, and their throats ache for water.

"Since lover boy spilled my canteen yesterday, we're plum out of anything good to drink," Shrift says. "We're gonna need some before we head off today."

Taurin shifts his body, uncomfortable with Shrift's accusation. "I didn't mean to. I was defending myself."

"Don't get yourself all flustered. The facts are what they are." Shrift stands, walks over to his leather bag, and slings the strap across his right shoulder. "We need water."

"Okay, so where can we get some?" Violet asks.

"We can find some on our way. I think I may know a spot or two, if they haven't all dried up by now."

"On our way to where?" Violet asks.

"Harbor Town," Shrift responds. "Get your stuff and let's get outta here before something realizes we're here."

"What's in Harbor Town?" Taurin asks.

"Answers. Now, quit squawking and put out that fire."

Taurin shoots Violet a quick glance. *Should we trust him?* he thinks. She nods. *Yes.* With that unspoken conversation, the two prepare to leave. Taurin kicks sand over the flames, extinguishing them, and Violet gathers what little supplies they have left: Taurin's leather satchel, which contains the items her father put in the bag, and the tablet. Violet puts her hand inside the satchel and her fingers brush against the tablet's thin glass. *Still there.*

"Ready," Violet says. "Let's get out of here."

Shrift pulls his copper goggles over his face, places his helmet on his head, and slips his long burlap coat over his shoulders. On his right hip rests his heat pistol, securely held in place by a leather holster; his left boot hides a crooked blade. "Better safe than sorry," he says before taking his first steps toward Harbor Town.

Taurin's white cotton shirt, ripped and worn from being chased and attacked, hangs like a loose sack on his frame. He hadn't thought he'd need much in the desert: a T-shirt, jeans, and a pair of sandals seemed like enough. Now, looking at Shrift with all his gear, he isn't sure he made the right choice.

Violet nudges Taurin with her hand. "Come on. We don't want to get left out here."

"I just wish we'd have thought to bring more than what we have."

"Here," Violet hands Taurin a khaki hat with a floppy, wide brim, and a blue bandana. "Shrift had a few odds and ends."

Taurin watches Violet as she passes him. On her head rests a hat similar to the one she just handed him. A purple bandana, stitched with a dozen white roses, covers her mouth. His leather satchel rests on her left shoulder. "I can carry that," he says, motioning to the leather bag. Violet doesn't respond and just keeps moving forward. With a few quick movements, Taurin ties the blue bandana around the back of his head and pulls it over his mouth. It makes it harder to breathe in the stale heat, but it will keep the sand from filling his lungs.

The sun rises high in the blue sky as the hours drip away like the liters of sweat from the travelers' bodies. This is truly a wasteland. The jagged mountains that blocked the sun for the first few hours of their journey eventually give way to miles of endless sand. Taurin keeps putting one foot after the other, pressing his feet into the scalding surface.

Deadly thirst itches at each of their throats. Shrift was right to be angry with Taurin for spilling the water; that simple mistake is magnified now under the burning sun.

Taurin coughs. "Are we close?" he asks. "We've been walking for hours."

"I know how long it's been," Shrift mumbles. He doesn't turn to address Taurin, but instead just keeps walking.

"Shrift, please," Violet says. "We have to stop. I need …" Her voice trails off and the world around her goes black. The sun is too hot, her throat is too dry, and her body can't stand it any longer. She hits the sand like a rag doll tossed from a tree.

"Violet!" Taurin yells. He kneels beside her and lifts her head up with his hands. "Wake up!"

Silent, Shrift moves to Violet, picks her up, and slings her over his broad shoulder, letting the satchel she carried fall to the ground. Taurin doesn't ask questions. He picks up the leather satchel and runs behind his leader, matching him stride for stride. Violet is in real trouble, and it doesn't matter who the hero is right now. Although Shrift has been anything but trustworthy so far, he's the only one who knows this desolate area. If Violet is going to survive, he's the one who will have to save her. The thought stings a little in Taurin's heart, but he doesn't dwell on it. The pace of the sprint and the cramping pain growing in Taurin's right side erase all his other feelings.

After a few minutes of nonstop running, Shrift stops and lays Violet on the sand.

"Are we here?" Taurin asks between heavy breaths. "Is there water somewhere close?"

Shrift ignores Taurin's words and walks over to a black stone that's sitting off to the right of the path. Smaller than one of Taurin's fists, the rock would be missed by anyone who didn't know exactly where to look. He flips the stone over and brushes away inches of collected sand to reveal a round, wooden lid. His steady hands pull the covering away. "It can't be!" Shrift yells.

Taurin rushes over and peers down at a dark hole in the sand—a well that's as deep as his body is tall, and just as wide, reveals itself to him. "It's empty," he says.

"Don't you think I know that?" Shrift snaps.

"Fine, let's just keep running until we get to the next one."

"There isn't a next one. If this one's empty, so is the next. It's over."

Taurin feels his eyes burning, and he grabs the collar of Shrift's coat, lifting him off the ground. "Listen to me. She's all I have, so you need to pull yourself together and figure something out." Heat builds in the tips of his fingers as anger stirs in his mind. "Do something," he spits.

"Let me go." Shrift shakes off Taurin's grip and reaches for his canteen. "I have an idea." He pulls it close to his ear and gives it a shake. "Good, there's a little left." He quickly unscrews the metal cap and then, with slight hesitation, steps over to Violet. "Take this," Shrift tells Taurin. He holds out the crooked blade with his left hand.

"What do you want me to do with that?" Taurin asks.

Shrift looks at Taurin, his blue eyes filled with bright-white flecks. "You need to make me bleed."

CHAPTER 12: OLD FRIENDS

SHIMMERS of light dance off the sharpened blade. Taurin, his hand curled around the knife's wooden handle, holds the pointed end against Shrift's tanned flesh. His forearm is soft, not calloused like the palms of his hands, and is exposed and ready for the cut. Violet lies flat against the sand, her lifeless eyes stare up at the boys without seeing them; they each played a part in causing her current condition, and now they must work together to save her.

"Do it," Shrift says. He takes a few deep breaths of the hot desert air in anticipation of the blade that doesn't come. "What are you waiting for? She needs this."

Taurin fixes his eyes on the knife and then looks down to Violet. She lies motionless like a wounded bird. In all the years he's know her, she's never been weak. Violet was the one who told him it would be all right when the flecks scorched his eyes; she was there when the others turned their backs on him. But now, when she needs him to be strong, he's frozen. "I don't think I can."

"Look at me." Shrift's eyes burn with white light. "Do what you've been wanting to do since we first met: cut me. I can't do it myself or I would."

"How do you know it will work?"

"Same way I know that your brother, Pulp, is chained to a wall and fighting hard just to keep breathing. Same way I know that you'd chop your own arm off instead of letting this little hummingbird die. Same way I know that if you don't start listening, I'm gonna split your head against that rock over there. Take that damn knife and cut me!"

Taurin slices the crooked blade through Shrift's forearm as easily as a fish glides through still water. Shrift winces at the pain, but he shakes his head and turns his focus to Violet. He pours the last few drops of water from the canteen into his palm, as a steady stream of liquid flows from his wound. Not blood, Taurin realizes—water. Clear and clean, the water flows from Shrift's arm into Violet's mouth. Taurin holds her lips open to make sure not a drop is wasted.

Violet's body jerks, and wet coughs, each more powerful than the last, wrack her body. Poofs of mist spray the sand and evaporate on contact. She blinks her heavy eyelids again and again, the glaring sunlight impossible to stand all at once.

"What happened?" Violet whispers. She turns her body to the side, looking over each of her companions. "Your arm, it's …"

"Ain't nothing but a scratch, darling," Shrift replies.

"I can't believe it worked!" Taurin exclaims. Pure, unfiltered joy rips through him, and he jumps up and throws his arms around the coarse fabric of Shrift's coat. He squeezes Shrift so tightly that his new companion couldn't get away if he tried. "You're a genius."

"What's gotten into you?" Violet asks, her mouth drops open in surprise and her brow furrows. "Did I miss something?"

Embarrassed, Taurin lets go of Shrift and steps over to Violet. "Sorry," he mutters. "I just didn't know what to do. You were so far gone, I panicked." He pauses for a moment, considering his words. "Shrift saved you."

Shrift's hand comes down hard against Taurin's back. "Hate to break up this priceless moment, but if it wouldn't bother you too much, I could use a bit of help." A thick stream of red blood pours from Shrift's arm. The jagged, rough wound would drain him in just a few minutes if left untreated.

"Taurin, you have to help him," Violet pleads.

A memory flashes in Taurin's mind. Always training him, Clue had left an apple by Taurin's home one day. Bruised and ugly, it wasn't anything someone would want to eat. A handwritten note beneath the fruit read:

Bring back what is spoiled.

Hold tight and make new.

"Bring back what is spoiled," Taurin repeats the phrase out loud. Crimson flecks grow and fill his eyes.

Violet smiles, remembering the event with the apple. "Hold tight and make new," she says, finishing the phrase. "You can do this."

Without hesitation, Taurin takes a hold of Shrift's arm. The cut pulses blood under his hand, coloring his fingers with red. "This may sting."

"Youch!" Shrift howls, dropping his guard for a moment and letting out a wild cry of pain. "You're burning me, you idiot!" He rips his arm away from Taurin's grip and curls his fingers into a fat fist. "I'm gonna knock you flat out!"

"You're welcome," Taurin says, a smile, wide and confident, stretching across his face. He glances at the now-sealed wound. "You can thank me later."

Shrift rubs his finger against his arm. Not a drop of blood is visible; not even a scar. "Great, now I'm probably infected with whatever you've got boiling inside of you." He moves to roll down his shirt's sleeve, but Violet stops him.

"What's that?" She points to an area on Shrift's exposed skin. A red circle with two faded letters marks the inside of his forearm, just below his bicep. "Looks like a *W* and an *F*."

Shrift quickly pulls down the rest of the sleeve. "Ain't nothing. Forget it."

Taurin's eyes narrow. "Brooks was right." He steps closer to Shrift. "The Watch Force had you, didn't they?"

Shrift rubs his arm, as if talking about the letters somehow brought back the pain. "It was a long time ago."

"You have to take us," Violet says. "That's where they're keeping Cay and Pulp."

"I'm a dead man if I go back."

"They're both dead if we leave them. Along with however many of us they have trapped there." Taurin points first to his own eyes and then to Shrift's. "Do you want whatever we are to end with me and you?"

"It's suicide. No one survives that place," Shrift says. "I swore I'd never go back. I got out by sheer luck, and I've been trying to avoid the Watch Force ever since."

"We will survive," Violet says. She stands and brushes the sand from her clothes. "We have to."

Grains of sand spin through the air in gentle cyclones, and the scorching sun shines down on the travelers. Although the companions' hearts race and sweat drips down their skin, no one says another word for some time. Violet and Taurin want to go where Shrift thought he'd never return to, and they know it must be his decision to take them there.

Shrift stands silent, rubbing his rough hands over the stubble on his square jaw. Taurin can see the indecision on his companion's face and silently hopes that he'll agree to help them, despite the risks. The Wasteland has hidden Shrift for some time, but if he agrees to help them, that protection will be over. Finally, slowly, Shrift speaks. "I'll help you."

"Shrift, you don't know what this means to us—" Violet begins, but Shrift holds up his hand to silence her.

"I'll help you, but it's gonna cost you."

"Anything," Taurin says. He crosses to stand in front of his friend with his hand outstretched. "Let's shake on it right here. Whatever you want, it's yours."

"Taurin, don't you want to see what he wants first?" Violet asks.

"It doesn't matter. I've got nothing left."

Shrift waves Taurin's hand off. "Not yet. You need to hear what I have to offer first. As usual, the lady is right." His bright smile fills his face, and a slow wink, directed at Violet, follows. "You're too quick to shoot. Need to know what you're aiming at first."

"I don't have time for a lecture," Taurin says. "Every second I waste talking to you is one less I can spend finding my brother. So, excuse me if I'm too fast to agree to whatever stupid demand you've cooked up in your head!"

Shrift throws up his hands in surrender. "Whoa there, no need to get worked up. I said I'd help you, and I will."

"Just tell me what you want, and it's yours," Taurin says.

Suddenly a rumble, low and loud, fills the air. Sand spins in the distance; someone or something is coming toward the travelers. Shrift reaches into his leather bag, pulls out a pair of black binoculars, and puts them to his eyes, pointing in the direction of the sand cloud.

"What is it?" Violet asks. Her heart flips and twists in her chest, and excitement pumps through her veins. Since she was young, she has always run toward the things that most people run away from. Stepping so close to the edge is how she's always felt most alive. Quick, unsteady breaths fill her lungs. "Can you see it?"

"No, but I know who it is."

"Who?" Taurin asks. He presses his fingers flat against his sweat-drenched forehead, narrowing his eyes to see, but it's no use. The sand is too thick and the distance too far. "I can't see anything.

Shrift sighs and hands Taurin the binoculars. Taurin stares into the chaos, waiting. Then the cloud of sand breaks for a moment and two bright red letters gleam back at him. Taurin suddenly feels as though all the air has been ripped from his lungs. Five black ash speeders emerge from the sandy cloud, each marked with the familiar *WF*, and each carrying an armed patrolman. "The Watch Force!" Taurin exclaims.

"This is bad," Shrift says. He scans the area and notices a collection of gray and black stones a couple hundred yards from the path. "Follow me!"

Violet grabs Taurin's arm and pulls him behind her as she runs. The sound is growing louder; the speeders are close. She sprints faster and faster until the black and gray rocks are right in front of her. The small pile of stones is not much taller than she is and won't offer much protection, but she trusts that Shrift has a plan. *He'd better.*

"Now what?" Taurin asks, breathing hard.

Flecks of white begin to fill Shrift's eyes as he stares at Taurin. "This isn't the way things were supposed to go, but I guess nothing can change that now. They've found us," he says.

"Watch Force," Taurin repeats. It feels like ages ago since he'd last met with the patrolmen. At least then, in the middle of the woods, he'd had his speeder; but here in the Wasteland, there are no twisted paths and overgrown trails to escape into. *We're trapped.*

Shrift picks up a glassy, diamond-shaped black rock about the size of a small apple and razor sharp on every side. "I got a plan. Just hide here and don't move a muscle."

"What's that for?" Taurin asks. "You can't knock them all off their speeders with one rock."

Shrift grabs the front of Taurin's shirt and pulls him close, his hot breath spilling onto Taurin's face. "Stay put and shut your mouth, or I swear this rock will be a permanent part of your skull. Got it?"

"Fine," Taurin says, pulling away. "But getting yourself killed isn't part of our deal. Got it?"

"Got it!" Shrift winks at Violet, then turns and races toward the oncoming cloud. The speeders haven't slowed down, and the sound of their engines shakes the ground. Violet and Taurin watch as their friend runs to the center of the road and waves his arms high above his head, the rock still held tightly in one fist. "Come and get me!" he yells.

CHAPTER 13: STANDOFF

THE SMOLDERING sun burns its bright rays across Taurin's face, causing him to squint. Through narrow eyes, he watches Shrift walk toward the approaching speeders. He'd offered to help, but been rejected. Shrift said that this was his fight and anyone else would just get in the way. At the time Taurin didn't have the energy to argue, and in some ways he's glad he didn't. His body aches and his mind throbs—he could use a break from the action. He lets loose a few long breaths and stretches his arms above his head. "Why can't we just have a normal day?" he asks.

"Because we're not normal," Violet replies, her eyes locked on Shrift. "None of us."

Five patrolmen reach for their heat pistols and Taurin considers Violet's words for a moment. *None of us*? Then, he looks back to Shrift and sees him lift a glassy stone above his head. The rock's razor-sharp edges dig into Shrift's skin and splatter the sand with drops of bright blood. Taurin knows this is part of the routine—becoming a part of the stone, but it's still difficult to watch.

The violent rumble of the speeders' engines rattle the sand. They are close to Shrift now, just a few yards away. Each carries a patrolman who has his heat pistol raised. The Watch Force have come to hunt, to kill, and he's just an obstacle in their way.

"Skin and bone turn to stone." The phrase clatters inside Taurin's head. With all their speed and force, he knows that the speeders will snap Shrift's body like a bag of dry twigs. Skin is soft. Bones are fragile. Stone is neither. It's easy to do something when your life isn't on the line, Clue had taught him as much, but focus takes far more effort when you're dealing with life or death. "Hurry up!" Taurin yells.

"Quiet," Violet scolds. "He knows what he's doing."

"Hope you're right." Once more Taurin watches as Shrift squeezes the jagged rock above his head, and once more he sees blood fall to the sand. This time, however, something is different. The winds calm and everything grows still for a moment. Then, he watches the transformation. Like a painter brushing long strokes of thick paint, Shrift's arms turn black, his skin becomes hard, and his muscles grow into sharpened boulders. "Flesh and bone have turned to stone."

"Finally," Violet says, wringing her hands.

Mesmerized, Taurin watches pieces of glass and metal spray into the air as a speeder collides with Shrift's stone body. The first patrolman doesn't have time to stop, and Shrift's hardened skin crumples the speeder like a scrap of paper on impact. The patrolman who had been riding the speeder meets a similar fate. His body lies broken and bloody against the sand.

"Look out!" Violet yells. "Behind you!"

With shocking power, Shrift turns and swings his heavy arms at the four remaining speeders. Metal clangs against stone, shattering on impact and shaking the ground. One after another, Shrift smashes and crashes his way through the next two patrolmen and their machines, ripping off fuel tanks and rubber tires like a wild animal devouring its prey. Black oil coats his face; Shrift looks like more like a beast than a man. Then, without warning, he stops moving.

The last patrolman quiets his speeder, steps off the machine, and aims his weapon at Shrift. A black helmet and dark visor cover his face. His pleated pants tuck tight into black leather boots. It's the same uniform Taurin saw in the temple. Even a red WF is stitched on the front of the suit jacket. Now, in the middle of the Wasteland, the Watch Force have returned.

Six bright flashes emerge from the patrolman's heat pistol, snapping Taurin back into the present. Each shot is precise and meets its target.

"Ahhh!" Shrift lets loose a wild shout before bringing his mammoth fists down on the patrolman's black helmet. Even from his hiding place, Taurin hears bones crack and sees blood spill. The patrolman goes limp and falls to the ground. Oil drips from Shrift's stone fists and silence blankets the Wasteland. There are no more enemies to fight, all is finally calm.

"Are you all right?" Violet asks, breaking the silence as she and Taurin emerge from their hiding spot. She looks at Shrift standing in the middle of the road. With hands of rock and legs of stone, he looks like a monster. To anyone else, Shrift would be terrifying, but Violet sees what he really is—a hero. She grips his jagged arm with her hand. "Are you in there, Shrift?"

"Can't believe you'd still touch me after watching me do what I just did. You're a strange girl," Shrift says. "Cute, but strange." He winks, and as fast as the black stone covered his body, it vanishes.

Taurin tosses a pair of khaki pants at Shrift. "Nice to see you're back to normal, but it's not nice to see *all* of you." He covers his eyes with his hands. "Please, put some pants on!"

"Nothing to be ashamed of," Shrift says. His words are strong, but the redness on his face reveals his true feelings. "Sometimes when I change I grow too much and destroy my clothes. Don't worry. I love the fresh air."

At first Violet hadn't noticed his nakedness. Moments ago, he was made of black boulders. Now, his tan skin is exposed … everywhere. She wants to speak and to look away, but her wide eyes and pinched lips won't allow her to do either. Shrift's broad shoulders are bound together by thick muscles. Although his arms and legs have returned to normal, they still look like they could have been chiseled from stone. Shrift's body is flawless. *Amazing*, Violet thinks.

"Ain't a peep show, little lady," Shrift says, grinning. His white teeth sparkle as his smile stretches from one cheek to the other.

The wind catches Violet's dark hair and whips Shrift in the face. "You just surprised me!" Violet yells, now looking away as heat rises in her cheeks.

"Yeah, I can have that effect."

"There's isn't anything I saw that's worth remembering." Violet walks over to stand by Taurin. Her chin points high toward the sky. "Where'd you get those pants you gave him?"

"From the bag," Taurin answers. "Your dad had them rolled up tight at the bottom."

"Good thing," Violet murmurs. "Let me know when you boys are ready to get going again. I just need a minute or two."

"Will do."

Violet walks past Taurin to the pile of stones where she had been hiding just minutes earlier. It's rare for her brain to be so mixed up, but right now her thoughts are like scrambled eggs. She needs time to relax, to sort her mind away from the boys. She sucks in a long, slow breath and exhales in a steady stream. "Feelings are for people without a purpose," her father loved to tell her. "You have a purpose, my dear, so use your brain and not your heart." It was easier back then to believe that, but now, in the midst of everything that's happening, it's hard to shut off her emotions. It would feel good to be held tight in Shrift's arms. To feel his strength wrapped around her. Her hands rub her stiff shoulders as gooseflesh crawls up her arms. *Just let it go.*

"That was a neat trick out there," Taurin says to Shrift. "I didn't know you had that in you."

"That's because you don't know me," Shrift says. Bent over, he sifts through the piles of debris on the road. Metal shrapnel, rubber tubes, and stands of electrical wire litter the area, but Shrift passes it all over without a second glance.

"You looking for something?" Taurin kneels down next to him. His hands start sifting through the debris. "I can help."

"As usual, you're too late." Shrift holds an object between his thumb and index finger. Sunlight glints off the silver finish. "I've taken care of it."

Taurin shakes his head. It was stupid to offer to help, but Shrift did just save his life. He thought maybe that act had changed things between them. It's clear now that it didn't. He squints and focuses on the small metal object. "Is that a key?"

"Not just any key. This here is very special." Shrift holds the small piece of metal in front of his lips and kisses it. "It's beautiful."

"Can I see it?" Taurin extends his arm and opens his hand.

"I suppose that's fair, being that you're the one gonna be needing it." Shrift presses the key into Taurin's palm. "Soak it in."

The key is short and fat, half the length of Taurin's pinky finger and wider than his thumb. The top is cut into four even sides, and a row of metal teeth extend out of the middle of the square. The letters *WF* are etched in the center of its top. "Watch Force," Taurin whispers.

"Ding! Ding! Ding!" Shrift's words make Taurin jump back. "You win the big prize, my friend."

"And what's that?"

"You're looking at her." Shrift, now standing, runs his hands down the back of an intact ash speeder. Except for silver handlebars and the red WF, flat black paint covers the entire machine. Even the wheels are painted to match the rest of the body. "I kept her pretty just for you."

"For me?" Taurin walks over and places his hand on the speeder's leather seat. Cool wind, rough roads, white knuckles, and countless other images flicker through his mind. He spent so many hours racing his own machine through the crooked paths that litter the areas near his home. Taurin built that speeder with his own hands, scavenging and bartering for parts whenever he got the chance, and then piecing them all together into something he called his own. It had saved his life more than once; more than once, it had almost taken it too. He'd give anything to have his speeder back, but just having the chance to ride one again will feel incredible.

"Try not to cry there, fella." Shrift's thick hand slaps Taurin's back. "Remember when I told you I needed something?"

Trying not to flinch or cry out in pain, Taurin bites his lower lip. The slap was both shocking and painful, but there is no way he's going to let Shrift think he can't handle it. He nods in answer to the question.

"Perfect! You're good with these things, right?"

"He's not good, he's great," Violet says. The leather satchel hangs off her right shoulder, and her head is covered with a thin beige-colored scarf. She rubs a thick cream on her arms, face, and legs once she stops next to the boys. "I was tired of being scorched, and I found some stuff in the bag."

Shrift smiles. "I knew *you* were the smart one."

"Someone has to be around here." Her shoulders straight, she walks past Shrift and hands Taurin the small container of cream. "Put some more of this on. The sun is getting hotter every second out here."

Taurin dips two fingers into the cream and rubs it over his exposed skin. He almost lets out a moan as the protective medicine seeps into his pores, soothing his skin. "I like the scarf." He points to the wrap around Violet's head. "Makes your eyes look," he searches for a word, "big."

"Thanks?" Violet shrugs. "It's just a piece of fabric I found in the bag."

"I didn't mean to say it like that." Taurin rubs his eyes. "My brain's just messed up."

Join the club, Violet thinks. "Let's just figure out what to do next."

Taurin nods. "Shrift was just showing me the speeder."

"She's a real beauty," Shrift says. "I made sure and kept her real nice. The heat pistol blasts would have killed a lesser man, but not me."

"We're both just glad you made it out intact." Violet catches her smile before it grows too big. "I'd hate to have to carry you the rest of the way."

Shrift's blue eyes lock onto Violet's. "I don't think I'd hate that. Not even a little."

"We're wasting time," Taurin says.

"Fair enough. I'm not proud of it, but I have a debt to repay in Harbor Town. It's not a little bit of money." He looks at Taurin. "If you help me take care of it, I'll take you to the Watch Force compound."

Violet eyes narrow. "What kind of debt?"

"The kind that slits your throat if it ain't paid."

"What's that have to do with me and the speeder?" Taurin asks. "You wanting me to sell it?"

"No. I need you to race it."

CHAPTER 14: A DEBT

TAURIN'S trained eyes scan every inch of the machine. His steady fingers twist and pull at each nut and bolt on the speeder. This is how he used to relax before the flecks dotted his eyes. He spent every spare moment of his childhood tinkering with and modifying all types of mechanical items. Some he meant to sell, but most he intended to keep. But his specialty and passion had always been ash speeders.

"You gonna ask her out on a date before you handle her like that?" Shrift asks.

"Hilarious," Taurin responds.

"Just wondering what the heck is taking you so long. You've been twisting and pulling for over an hour. Need to get a move on before we die of heat stroke."

"I have to make sure it's safe to drive. Otherwise we'll end up a different kind of dead."

Violet walks around each side of the speeder. Though not as skilled as Taurin, she has seen her fair share of machines like this. She grew up shoulder to shoulder with him; what he did, she did. Before Taurin's flecks appeared, they spent hours digging through piles of scrap metal and wires. It was fun to find the right piece for a speeder they were working on, or even better, to find a part worth its weight in coin. "Looks like the back tire needs air."

Taurin walks to the rear of the speeder and kneels down. He grips the tire in his hand and squeezes. "Soft."

"Thought so." She smiles and tilts her head to one side.

Taurin looks to Violet and for an instant is carried away. Her eyes are what snag him. So many times he's stared into them and seen nothing but the eyes of a friend. Now, their chocolate color is different, alluring. If only it were just the two of them, then maybe he'd have a chance; but it isn't, and he doesn't. At least, that's what his head is telling him. Their time in the forest is behind them now. It's better to move on than linger in the past. He looks down to examine the machine. "You're right. It's low."

"You mean to tell me that even after I kept it so pretty by getting blasted in the chest, it still won't work?" Shrift gives his head a violent shake and kicks piles of sand into the air. "Just my luck!"

"Relax," Taurin says. "How far is it to Harbor Town?"

"Maybe a two-hour drive on the back of that piece of junk." He spits a glob of saliva at the speeder. "Otherwise, we need to make camp before the sun fades. Unless you'd rather freeze to death, that is."

Taurin takes a slow breath, thinking. The tire is low and getting lower by the second. An almost invisible cut in the outer rubber is leaking air. He licks the tip of his finger and holds it close to the puncture. The light breeze from the cut tickles the moisture on his skin. "It's a slow leak, but it won't carry us all very far."

"Great," Shrift moans. "Guess we need to look for shelter, cause we ain't making it anywhere on foot. Not with no water."

"No need. We're all making it to Harbor Town. Today," Violet says. She walks to Taurin and looks him straight in the eyes. "What was broken can be fixed."

The phrase resonates with Taurin. One morning, a couple weeks earlier, he had found a note and a metal chain by his front door. The chain's bottom link was slit down the middle—broken. Clue's handwriting covered the torn paper.

What was broken can be fixed.

What was taken can be returned.

As always, the note's instructions didn't make sense at first. Yes, he'd formed fire before, but he'd never done much else with his touch. He'd spent hours with the chain that day, but nothing more than sparks and smoke came from his fingers. Then, sometime during the night, Taurin cleared his mind and held the chain in his hand. Instead of focusing on himself, he concentrated on the metal instead. The countless strands of silver came alive in his mind, and he saw what to do. He fused several shredded microscopic tears together and the chain became whole again. At the time, it was the most impressive and most difficult task he'd completed. The action, though similar to calling fire, drained far more energy, however. For hours he was spent—exhausted, weak, and useless. "I remember."

"You can do this." Violet's eyes narrow. Her face fills with a vibrant smile. "I know you can."

Any doubts in his mind about what he needs to do are erased with Violet's words. She'd always been the one to push him. The thought of letting her down had often been his sole motivation to keep trying, no matter the cost. "Okay," he says, "but if I pass out or something, don't let Shrift near me."

Violet giggles. "It's a deal."

"You'll be laughing when I leave you in the sun to cook," Shrift mutters.

Taurin's lips curl into half a smile, and he places his hand on the tire. "I wouldn't expect any less." The dark rubber sizzles hot against his palm. The coarse sand and dirt filling the tire treads grind at his skin. Taurin shuts his eyes and clears his mind, but his worries and fears fog the process. Focus on the pain. *The burn*, he tells himself.

He feels the small rip in the tire, and countless microscopic scraps of dark material consume his mind like a torn puzzle. Piece by piece, he pulls the shreds together in his mind, mending them until the hiss of the leak stops. Finished, he thinks. But then, a tremor rattles Taurin's body, and the color drains from his face. His bright-blue eyes go dim, and his body crumples against the sand.

"Taurin!" Frantic, Violet's hands smack his face. She leans down and hovers her cheek above his lips. "Wake up," she whispers. His soft, warm breath tickles her skin, causing her to shiver. Taurin blinks slowly.

"Shrift, bring me some water," Violet says.

"Ain't got much left, so be careful."

Violet snatches the tin canteen from Shrift's hand without a response. She knows this is the last of the water and doesn't need to be reminded. *Selfish*, she thinks. She carefully unscrews the lid and pours small drops on Taurin's cracked lips. His tongue reflexively licks the water and pulls it into his mouth.

"That's good," Taurin says. His voice, though soft, is clear. "Don't give me too much. We'll need it." He sits up and stretches his lean arms over his head. A painful ache throbs in his skull. Just as he expected, fixing the tire had taken most of his energy. "Did it work?"

Violet leans down and presses her finger against where the rip had been. No wind. No sound. Not even a ridge from a patch or repair. "It's like it was never there."

"What once was broken," Taurin says. "It's like Clue knew what would happen."

"I think he was just preparing you for anything."

"Or maybe he knew more than we think." Taurin looks at Violet, his eyes steady and focused. Maybe it's the heat or the excitement of the moment, but he's certain he sees a shade of red cover her cheeks.

"Time to quit cooing and get moving," Shrift says. "Unless you think he needs mouth-to-mouth."

Violet stands and slams the tin container against Shrift's chest. "Don't be a jerk." She bends over and digs through the leather satchel until she finds the small container that held the jam her father had made. She twists the lid open, and the sweet smells of berries and flower blossoms cause her mouth to water. Just a small amount remains of the jam; it's not enough to share. She hands Taurin the container. "You need to eat all of this. Don't argue with me."

Taurin may have argued with Violet another time, but not now. His dusty fingers dip into the purple jam, and he shoves the sticky substance into his mouth. It's not much, but it's enough to send a rush of energy back through his body. "I needed that," he says, twisting the lid back on the container and handing it to Violet. "Thanks."

"It's just peachy that you're feeling better, but if we get to Harbor Town after dark, then we might as well slit our own throats. Get my drift?" Shrift glares at Taurin. "So grab your gear and let's roll."

"Just wait a minute," Violet says, tucking long strands of dark hair behind her right ear. Her brown eyes, filled with questions, glare at Shrift. "How do we know?"

Shrift straightens his shoulders and frowns. Dark hairs on his arms bristle. Violet's question caught him off guard. Not the words, but the tone. "Know what?"

"It's just that Harbor Town seems more dangerous than you first said. Especially now that we know the Watch Force is on our trail. We're risking a lot."

"Well, that's my deal. So take it or shove it."

"It's our best chance," Taurin says. "Shrift's the only one who knows where Pulp and Cay are."

"That's just it. How do we know he's telling the truth?"

Shrift pulls off the leather glove that covers his right hand. With quick, angry movements, he twists the sleeves of his coat and shirt into a single, tight roll just below his elbow. A dark circle the size of a small fist, with the letters *WF* in the middle, marks his inner arm. "Happy now?"

The mark, crude and scarred, looks to have be placed with a hot brand and never treated after the burn. Thick, gray scar tissue covers where the scalding iron pressed against his soft flesh. It's impossible, but for a moment Violet almost swears she can still smell the char. "Did they do that to you?"

"Was a long time ago." Shrift pulls his sleeve back down to cover the mark. "They did worse than that, so believe me when I tell you I remember where to go. I remember." His voice trails off and his eyes look away for a few moments. The sand and wind have made his skin hard in the Wasteland, but the memories that haunt his mind can still steal his strength in a second.

"I'm sorry," Violet says. "I didn't know."

Shrift shrugs. "Ain't nothing but the past. Can't change it by being sorry about it."

"Shrift is right. We all wish we could change something that's happened, but we can't." Taurin says. "Let's head out before the past catches up with us."

"What about the speeder?" Violet asks. "Won't people think we're with the Watch Force with the speeder's paint job?"

"I know a guy in Harbor Town who can make that all go away. For a price, of course," Shrift says. "We can park it outside the town and let him know where to find it."

"So, you trust this guy?" Violet asks.

"Not really, but I don't trust anyone in that place. It's full of killers and deadbeats."

"So you'll fit right in." Taurin smiles and slugs Shrift on his left shoulder. "Get your gear and let's go. We'll deal with the murderers and thieves once we get there."

Shrift walks to the speeder and slings his long legs over the seat, his gloved hands grip the handlebars. He presses his leather boots against the front foot pegs. "What you waiting for?"

Taurin crosses his arms. "I thought I was the one who was supposed to be driving. Isn't that what you wanted?"

"You thought wrong. No need to waste your talents yet."

"Just get on, Taurin." Violet slips in behind Shrift. "Don't get any ideas. Got it?" she says, wrapping her arms around his waist.

"I got it just fine, darling." Shrift flashes her a toothy grin. "Get on or we'll leave without you, Taurin. I'm sure there's enough room on the back."

Taurin grumbles. The sight of Violet so close to Shrift twists his stomach into knots. *It's stupid to be jealous*, he tells himself, but he still can't stop grinding his teeth. None of the leather seat remains for him, so he has to hop on the tail end of the speeder. Just a molded piece of painted metal separates him from the rubber tire. "Perfect," he mumbles.

"Scoot up," Violet says. "There's plenty of room if you put your arms around me."

Before Taurin can move, Shrift starts the speeder and twists the throttle. The machine roars to life, sending the three travelers speeding down the sand-covered roadway. Taurin grips the metal under his legs; the sharp ridge digs into his palms. It would be a challenge to hold on under normal speeds, but Shrift has no plan to slow down. The sun is already starting to dip low in the sky. If night arrives in Harbor Town before they do, it could mean the end of the journey—the end of everything.

VIOLET

CHAPTER 15: ROLFF

THE ORANGE light of the sun splits into vibrant shades of purple and pink as the day sets into evening. Soon darkness will paint the landscape. Shrift pushes hard against the throttle, as if willing the machine to move faster, but it's no use. The weight of the three travelers strangles the speeder's power. Though no longer leaking air, the rear tire still isn't as firm as it needs to be to maximize speed. "Almost there!" Shrift shouts. "Hang on!"

"Like we have a choice!" Taurin yells. Two hours of unbalanced turns and erratic braking has made it clear why Shrift needs someone else to race the speeder. The machine has controlled him the entire trip, forcing his hand one way or the other. To win a race, the driver needs to be in control. Countless broken roadways and tangled forest trails have taught Taurin how to manipulate such a powerful speeder. Just the thought of placing his hands on the throttle sends a rush of excitement through his body and brings a smile to his face.

"Look!" Violet says, unwrapping her hand from around Shrift's chest to point. "Is that what I think it is?"

Shrift releases the throttle and squeezes the handbrake, bringing the speeder to stop. He twists the key and quiets the machine's engine. He pulls the goggles off his face and rubs his eyes. Rugged, untamed mountains stretch for miles across the endless horizon. Each fractured edge and piercing peak look to have been sharpened with a whetstone. A narrow path made of crushed black rock leads toward the center of the mountains.

"Where are we?" Taurin asks.

"You said you wanted to go to Harbor Town, didn't you? This is how we get there," Shrift says.

"We're going in there?" Taurin asks.

"Only way," Shrift responds. "Unless you wanna go up and over." He motions to the mountain peaks.

"Piles of broken glass would be easier to climb."

"Thought so." Shrift swings his legs off the speeder and stretches. "Get off and help me stash this thing."

"Where are we going to hide it?" Violet asks. "There's nothing here but sand."

"Then you better start digging."

"Hilarious." Violet climbs off the speeder and walks toward the entrance to Harbor Town. Jagged boulders frame a tight roadway that's just wide enough to fit a pair of speeders side by side. The path goes forward into the belly of the mountains for a hundred feet until it stops at a ten-foot-tall, olive-green metal door. Three red slashes are painted on the front of the door, as if a giant creature had clawed the metal. "What's that from?" She points to the markings.

"Not *what*, darling. It's *who*." Shrift's usual casual smile is missing. His tone and his body are rigid.

"We can talk about what or who later," Taurin says. "I'm too tired to die tonight, so let's just leave the speeder here and hope your friend finds it in time. That work?" Shrift doesn't respond. He stands silent, staring at the three red claw marks on the green door. "Shrift, did you hear me?"

"I heard ya," Shrift says, his voice quiet but hard. "So did half of Harbor Town. Just shut your mouth and do it already." He turns and walks out of the entrance and back onto the sand. The sun is just a pink sliver against the horizon. The moon, full and round, sits high in the sky.

"What crawled up his butt?" Taurin whispers to Violet. "One minute he's all smiles, the next he's off sulking."

"Sounds like someone else I know." Violet nudges Taurin with her elbow. "Just push the speeder as far off to the side as you can and let's get into town."

"Fine, but I *don't* act like him."

"Whatever." Violet runs her fingers through her hair, sending sand flying in all directions. She covers her mouth as three dry coughs escape her throat. The sound, both loud and forceful, echoes down the path, stopping at the doorway.

"WE DON'T WANT ANY!" A loud voice yells from behind the door. "LEAVE OR DIE!"

Violet's hands spring up and cover her mouth. She looks from the door to Shrift, her eyes wide with fear. Taurin stands frozen with one hand on the speeder and the other pushed flat against the mountainside. He also looks to Shrift for answers.

"Useless," Shrift mumbles, shaking his head. He hurries to the door and then cups his hand around his mouth and shouts, "Let me in, you fat pig!"

"NO, IT CAN'T BE! YOU'RE DEAD!"

Shrift pulls off his helmet and looks toward the top of the door. He flashes a huge smile, though his teeth are still smeared with bug guts from driving the speeder, and raises his arms in the air. "I'm not dead, you brainless sack of goat guts. Let me in!"

"HA, HA! IT IS YOU!"

A violent burst of air fires sand against Shrift's face, knocking him on his back. The shrieking sound of metal raking against solid rock causes him to cover his ears; Taurin and Violet cover their ears in turn. After a few painful seconds the sound stops, and the olive-colored door that once blocked the way is now a seamless part of the black mountain.

"I was sure you were a sack of spoiled meat in the desert by now," the voice blurts from behind the clouds of sand. "But here you are!"

"Pipe down, you blubbering idiot. I don't want everyone to know I'm here." Shrift stands and shakes his head in an attempt to stop the ringing in his ears. "You really need to get the hydraulics fixed on that door."

"A little loud for your liking? The desert has made you soft. I swear it has!" Almost as round as he is tall, a short man with a fat belly steps though the cloud. A thick red beard twists into tight curls against his portly face. In one hand he holds a silver-plated heat rifle that is longer than he is tall. A telescopic scope, half the length and twice the width of the rifle, is fitted on top. The weapon shimmers from the bright light shining through the now-open entrance. It's both beautiful and deadly.

A fat fist slams into Shrift's belly, pushing all the air from his lungs in a single blow. He gasps and hunches over in pain. "You little …"

"See, I told ya! SOFT! Ha, ha!"

Taurin, fists clinched, rushes to Shrift's side. Crimson burns in his eyes and smoke rises from his palms. "Step away from my friend and I might not hurt you."

"You didn't tell me you brought a little friend," the fat man says. "And not just any friend from the looks of it."

"He's no one," Shrift says. "Just some dumb kid I picked up in the desert." He steps in front of Taurin to block his path and shoves him back, giving him a warning glare. "Stay away." His eyes, narrow and stern, say the rest.

"I thought you were in trouble," Taurin whispers. "I was just trying to help."

"I'm not, so stop trying."

"Shrift, my boy. Aren't you going to introduce me to your special friend?" Pulling on his unkempt beard with fingers the size of sausages, the fat man pushes by Shrift and walks straight to Taurin. "He seems like someone I need to know." The man's pale green eyes study the boy. "Interesting."

Taurin steps back and raises a pair of clenched fists, watching him warily, looking for something that might give away his intentions. A hand-stitched, leather vest fits tight around the man's round belly. Rows of silver bullets, each over an inch long, cross his short, wide chest. A green metal helmet that's gouged with rusted bullet holes sits crooked on top of his braided red hair that stretches to just above his thick thighs. "I don't want any trouble," Taurin says.

"What you want isn't what you've got," the fat man says, taking a step toward Taurin. "Trouble always follows your kind." The man's hot breath, stinking of onions and milk, spills over Taurin's face as his moves closer. He curls his cracked red lips back and grinds his yellow teeth. "Just a matter of how fast you can run."

"That's enough, Rolff," Shrift says. "I told you he's nothing, and I meant it." Shrift shoves the man to the ground and presses a black boot hard against his belly. "We can do this without you, but it would be easier with you. Don't matter to me one way or the other. You choose."

"Lies!" Rolff shouts. "You've brought death to me!" He squirms underneath Shrift's boot, but it's useless. "That one is marked, just like you!" Rolff shakes a fist at Taurin. "They'll find him, and then they'll kill me for knowing about him. It's bad enough that I knew one Organic. Now I know two."

Shrift pushes harder against Rolff's stomach. "Watch your words, friend, or the murdering bastards who are following us will be too late to kill you. Understand?" He grinds the tread of his boot against the man, who groans beneath Shrift's weight.

Rolff gives a wild nod. "Yes. Yes. Just let me up!"

"Fine, but you swear to me on your mother's life that you won't tell anyone about my friend?"

"I swear it!" Rolff puts both of his hands against the boot and shoves it away from him. He exhales a long stream of air and lays his head flat against the sand. "You're still as crazy as when they threw you out of here."

"That's why we make great friends." Shrift extends a hand to help Rolff up. "Quit being lazy. We have work to do."

"Don't take my growing belly as a sign that I've become lazy, my friend." He grabs a hold of Shrift's hand and pulls himself off the ground. "I've just been bored since you left."

"And hungry, it looks like," Shrift says.

"I sit at the door all day and shoot those who try to break in. What do you expect me to look like?"

"You don't look bad to me," Violet says sweetly, approaching Rolff cautiously. "A real man needs to be strong out here in the Wasteland to help those who aren't tough enough." She wraps her hands around his bicep and squeezes. Out of the corner of her eyes she catches a glimpse of Taurin shaking his head. *He has his powers, and I have mine,* she thinks.

Rolff's puffy cheeks turn red, matching his bright beard. "Yes," he says. "Plenty tough to protect someone as lovely as you."

"I'm sure you are, but are you clever enough to help me with a job that these boys can't?"

"Anything!" Rolff says, looking surprised at his own words. "I mean, I can try."

"See that ash speeder over there?"

"Yeah, I see it."

"Well, Shrift said he knew someone who could help us make it look a little less …"

"Stolen?" Rolff crosses his wide arms in front of his chest. "That's a Watch Force speeder."

"We didn't steal it," Taurin blurts.

"Does it matter?" Violet asks, her hands on her hips. "I mean, who cares how we got it? This is the Wasteland! Thieves and murderers make their homes just beyond that metal door, and we've come to find them. Rolff isn't afraid of a little danger; are you?"

"I like her. She reminds me of a fiery girl I once knew," Rolf says, grinning.

"It's settled then." Violet pats Rolff on the shoulder and heads toward the open door. "We'll need it finished by tomorrow morning."

"What?" Rolff asks. "That isn't enough time, and you haven't given me any coin for the job."

"You'll have your money if my friend here wins the race tomorrow," Violet says, gesturing to Taurin. "So, if you want anything other than a handshake, I'd throw a couple new tires on to make sure that thing is race-worthy."

"But, I …"

"It's no use, you soft-bellied slug. She's prettier than you and a whole lot smarter too. I'd just do as she says and be glad she didn't ask for more," Shrift says as he walks by Rolff.

"But …"

"Don't feel bad," Taurin says. "She's smarter than us too."

CHAPTER 16: HARBOR TOWN

A GRAY fog hovers above rows of rusted lanterns that shine a pale light on metal shacks, crumbling brick buildings, and an endless amount of dirty brown water that curves along the northern tip of the city. Once a beautiful ocean, the bay is now a stagnant reminder of the filth that has covered the area for decades. Three ancient processing plants sit idle and abandoned on the water's edge, still carrying the stench of a lifetime of raw refining materials. Six massive smoke stacks, made of red brick and gray mortar, tower over the scraps of habitation below. A single gravel roadway winds through Harbor Town like a snake. It's the only road in or out.

"This is Harbor Town?" Taurin asks.

"What did you expect?" Shrift responds. "A parade?"

"Not this."

Violet pushes past Taurin and sniffs the warm air. She scans the makeshift buildings pieced together with corrugated metal and chiseled, black rocks from the mountains. A stream of filth flows freely next to the roadway, emptying into the murky ocean. Birds covered in black feathers circle above the town. "It's perfect."

Shrift grins at her response. "This place is filthy and the people are rotten, but it's one of the only places I feel comfortable. Thieves and killers don't bother me. I know where they stand. I'm an outcast just like everybody else here. These rusted shacks and filth covered streets are my only real home," he pauses, then shakes his head. "Follow me, or sleep in the ditch. It doesn't matter to me."

"Where are we going?" Taurin asks. "It looks like this place is abandoned."

"Not quite," Violet says. "Look over there." She points down the road to a brick building with a roof made of patched metal. It looks much like the rest of the town, save for a large neon sign that blinks *DRINK HER* over the entrance. It would say *DRINK HERE,* but the last E is dark; the bulb likely burnt out long ago. Two gray metal doors block the entrance, and an armed guard stands watch in front of building. His slouching posture and soggy eyes suggest he's in desperate need of rest, or that he drank too much of whatever is being served inside the pub. "You know him?" Violet asks Shrift.

"Yeah, he seems like your kind of guy." Taurin smirks.

Shrift doesn't respond, but Taurin notices that the white flecks in his eyes flicker as he watches the guard. The man's skintight leather pants and jacket show off his thick muscles. His paw-like hands sport fat knuckles, still bloody from a recent fight, and callouses from what Taurin assumes are countless others. An old heat pistol is strapped to his left leg, and a white, circular patch with three red claw marks covers the right shoulder of his black jacket. He doesn't look like someone to be tested in any state of consciousness.

"Let's keep moving," Shrift finally says.

"I thought you knew this place," Taurin says. "We need to rest, and this looks like our only option."

"What do we have here?" a strange voice asks from behind the travelers. "Take them."

A club or something equally fierce smacks into the back of Taurin's head, sending him crashing into the spilt stone that makes up the roadway. Shrift and Violet, met with the same strike to their heads, lie next to him, their cheeks and lips bloody from the impact. Taurin's own face feels sticky against the gravel, but whether it's from blood or something in the rocks, he doesn't know. The travelers are silent. The hard end of a heat rifle makes sure of that.

"Pathetic," the voice spits. "Bring them inside the pub."

A piercing sound screams inside Taurin's head. He instinctively brings his hands up to cover his ears, but the noise only grows louder. "Stop!" he yells. "Please!"

"Stop what?" the voice asks. "I wasn't doing anything."

As quickly as it began, the sound fades to nothing, and Taurin opens his eyes to familiar surroundings. To his left is a simple wall built from gray concrete blocks; his brother, Pulp, sits on a woven bed mat on his right. Taurin blinks once and rubs his face with spread fingers.

Pulp rises and hurries to Taurin's side, his footsteps heavy on the flooring. He squeezes Taurin's shoulder with long, thick fingers. "Nightmares again?" he asks, shaking his head. "It's those damn flecks. Father was right; they're a curse."

Taurin stares at his brother, who sits next to him. Pulp is tall and built like a boulder. His thick, wavy, almond-colored hair is disheveled from sleep, and a hint of dark stubble colors his jaw. Pulp's brown eyes, though the right shape and size, look different than Taurin remembers. The sparkle of life that always shone in them is missing. "You aren't Pulp," Taurin whispers. "You're just a reflection." He scans the room once more. "This isn't …"

"Real?" Pulp says, but the voice isn't his own. Pulp's body melts away like ice left in the sun, and is replaced with the shadow of a girl with long hair. "It was easier this time. You made it that way."

"Echo?"

"Yes, I've been wanting to speak with you, but your mind hasn't been free until now."

"I've been busy."

The girl's body shifts into view more clearly. Her skin is as white as porcelain beneath wild strands of dark-red hair. Her green eyes shimmer like emeralds above her sharp, narrow nose. "You're here now, and that is what matters."

"Why can I see you?" Taurin runs his fingers through Echo's hair. It's soft and smooth, and the strands feel like silk. "I mean, if this really is you."

Echo pushes him away, her thin hand tipped with sharp, pointed fingernails. "You can see me now because I trust you."

"You didn't before?"

"That isn't what matters. When will you be here?"

Taurin scoots against the wall, a bit taken back by the bluntness of the question. The rough concrete bricks feel the same against his back as they did in his house back at home, but they offer little support. In the back of his mind, he knows they aren't really there—Echo's not there. It's all just some sort of messed-up trance or dream. Still, to be in his own room again, even an imaginary version, feels strangely comforting. "Is my brother okay?"

A few seconds of silence pass. Echo pulls two large handfuls of her wavy red hair behind her head and twists them into a ponytail, then fixes her bright-green eyes on him. "I wish I had better news, but I don't. Your brother is in real danger."

"What does that mean?" Beads of sweat drip down Taurin's forehead and fall onto his bed mat. He reaches for Echo once more, but she leans away from him. "Just tell me if he's hurt!"

"You mustn't touch me in this place," Echo says, her words strong and deliberate. "Do not try to touch me again, or it will all be over. Do you understand?"

"No, I don't! How could I understand any of this?"

"I am sorry, but there is much to tell you and so little time. Just know that more of us are killed every day. If you don't hurry, your brother will soon meet the same fate."

"I'm doing all I can, but—"

"Do more," Echo interrupts. "Do everything you can to make it here by the week's end, or you will arrive too late."

The same painful burst of sound explodes inside Taurin's mind, causing him to curl into a ball on the mat. White light bursts behind his eyelids. A feverish ache rolls through his body. Sweat pours down his face, and violent tremors rock him back and forth on the ground. *This isn't a dream*, he realizes. *This is real.*

"Get that scum off my wooden floor before he stains it with his fluids," a deep voice says. "He's been out far too long. Wake him." A pair of powerful hands lift Taurin several feet in the air. First fear rushes through him, then pain. The hands that hold him, wrapped in tight black leather, release him again, and Taurin falls against the wooden floor planks with such force that it shakes the room. A glazed vase rattles off a shelf and shatters on the ground.

Taurin manages to open a swollen eye and examine his surroundings. He looks for Violet and Shrift but they are missing. A short, thin man stands just a few feet from Taurin's face. His feet are bare, clean, and well-manicured, and a white, sleeveless cotton tunic covers the rest of his body but reveals a pair of hulking biceps. His smooth, shaven head shines under the bright lights. His single blue eye sits to the left of his fat, crooked nose. Three red scars cover the area where his other eye should be. The pattern is one Taurin has seen before. "Claw," Taurin says, his voice just a whisper.

"Gifted *and* intelligent. This truly is my lucky day." The bald man extends a hand down to Taurin. "Take it. I won't harm you."

"Too late," Taurin says, wiping blood from his busted lip. "Your friend over there already took care of that." He motions to the guard who he had seen earlier slouching against the bar's doorway. Now he stands upright behind Taurin, his massive arms crossed across his puffed chest and a vacant look painted on his face.

"That's just one of my men. Unlike you and me, he is a dog that needs to be better trained." The bald man pulls a fat cigar made of brown leaves that form tight spirals around ground tobacco, from a narrow pocket stitched on the side of his tunic, and motions for the guard to lean down. "Cut it," he commands.

The guard pulls a small pocket knife from his jacket, leans down, and slices the pointed tip off the cigar.

"Light it."

With one quick motion, the large man removes a match from his pocket, strikes it against his jaw, and lights the cigar.

"Now, give me your hand."

Without hesitation, the guard extends his palm. The bald man presses the burning end of the cigar into his guard's palm. It sizzles against his flesh, releasing an acrid smell into the air, but he doesn't flinch.

"I don't need to see this," Taurin says, covering his mouth and nose with his hand. "I know who you are."

The bald man says nothing as he walks past Taurin to his desk on the opposite side of the room. A golden knife with a serrated, hooked blade rests on top of it. He picks it up and walks past Taurin once more to stand directly in front of the guard. The cigar still smolders in the man's palm, but he stands rigid.

"You may have heard of me, boy, but you do not know who I truly am." With one quick swipe, the bald man slices the jagged blade into his guard's neck, cutting through the skin with ease. Thick like syrup, blood gushes from the wound and spills on the floor. The guard drops to his knees and presses his large hands against his neck, but it's no use. It's only a matter of seconds before he collapses into a pile of muscle and blood-stained leather.

Flecks of crimson burn in Taurin's eyes. His shoulders shake, and the hair on his arm bristles. "You're a monster."

"I am *many* things," the bald man says. Then, he picks up a tiny silver bell and rings it three times. The metal door at the back of the room swings open and, like trained dogs, two more guards enter the room. They are built and dressed just like the dead man on the floor. "He failed."

The guards give a silent nod and, with an unspoken understanding, take ahold of the lifeless man's shoulders and pull him through the open door. A red stain smears the ground and disappears out of sight as they slam the door shut behind them. The bald man then kneels next to Taurin. "My name is Claw. It's a pleasure to meet you."

Anger boils beneath Taurin's skin. Power surges inside him, causing his fingers to twitch. He could kill Claw with a stream of orange flames, but that would accomplish little. Shrift and Violet are missing, and Claw is the key to their safe return. Taurin takes a deep breath, stands, and brushes the dust from his shirt and pants.

"You're right. I don't know you, but I'd like to." The words are like acid in his mouth, each burning more than the last.

Claw appears happy with Taurin's response and stands, flexing his biceps. He runs a single hand over his bald head as if to straighten invisible strands of hair. "Please, take a seat."

A delicate-looking wooden chair is positioned in front of Claw's desk. It's back and legs are made from a collection of woven tree branches, each one stained and polished to match the cherry color of the floors. A rough black stone acts as the chair's seat. Taurin examines it, looking for clues of potential malice. After a moment, however, he sits. To his surprise, the tangled branches do not crush his body to dust; they actually feel quite good against his sore back.

"I'm sorry for calling you a monster," Taurin says, rehearsing the words first in his mind. "Everything just happened so fast."

Claw picks up the cigar from the floor and places it between his lips. The ground tobacco was extinguished by the guard's blood and no longer smolders beneath the brown leaves. Claw raises his index finger in front of the cigar and whispers, "Burn bright with flesh. Light the night." A small, blue flame leaps from the tip of his finger and lights the leaves again. Then the man turns his attention to Taurin. "Seems you were right, my boy. I *am* a monster."

CHAPTER 17: CONVERSATIONS

CLAW sits on the edge of his desk, drawing long puffs on his shrinking cigar. The blue flame on his fingertip has been extinguished, but for Taurin, its memory still hangs in the air like the gray tobacco smoke spilling from Claw's mouth. "So, you are an Organic?"

The word *Organic* hangs heavy in the room. Taurin's heard it before, but coming from Claw, it sounds twisted and menacing. It's a difficult task to conceal crimson flecks and smoke-tipped fingers, so to have a stranger know his secret so quickly is unexpected and unwanted. "I don't really know what that means."

Claw leans toward Taurin, blowing the scent of burnt tobacco in his direction. "Do you want to?" he asks. Slow and careful, he stands and walks around Taurin's chair. The floor's redwood planks creak and moan under his bare feet.

"I just want to find my brother," Taurin says. "He's been taken, and they'll kill him if I don't do something." The words fall too easily from his mouth. He'd planned to lie to Claw, but the truth just slipped out. "They think he's me."

Lost in thought, Claw stares up at the wooden beams that brace the metal ceiling, absently blowing puffs of smoke into the air. "I assume you mean the Watch Force?"

Taurin nods.

"They hate us, those men in the dark, pleated suits. I've seen them rip children from their beds and smash the skulls of the mothers who resisted," Claw says.

"You saw them and lived? I thought I was the only one."

"Yes, I thought the same thing. And now, here we are." Claw draws a final pull from the cigar. The fire burns down to the end until there is nothing but a pile of smoldering ash left. "Strange, don't you think?"

A lump forms in Taurin's throat. This man, Claw, makes his skin crawl. It was just minutes ago that he slit the guard's throat and let him bleed to death on the floorboards. Now, he speaks as a friend who knows a secret he wants to share, or perhaps to pry free. *You've said too much. Just breathe*, Taurin thinks. He takes a few deep breaths until he finds the right words. "What do you want from me?"

"It's refreshing to hear such a blunt question. Most people are too afraid or too mindless to ask me anything of importance."

"Can you blame them? I mean, you just ordered your men to carry out a dead body like it was a bag of garbage."

"True. It is my own fault that they are afraid. Yet, that fear is what keeps this town alive. Without it, without me, everyone here would be dead. You are young, so such things are hard for you to understand."

"You're right." Frustrated, Taurin stands and locks his hands into fists. "I don't understand any of this, and it's time you told me what's going on!"

Like a bolt of lightning, Claw crosses to the boy and presses his blade, still wet with the dead guard's blood, against Taurin's shirt. "Do not take my respect for you as a sign of weakness, boy," Claw hisses. "I may need you, but I can find another way to accomplish what I desire. DO NOT TEST ME AGAIN!"

Taurin's muscles tense and his pulse throbs. Pure, focused rage boils in his belly. The tip of Claw's blade is pressed against him, but that isn't what angers him. He knows he could kill Claw with a single thought, and for the first time, he wants to. He can see the flames and feel the heat within him. It would be easy. It would be fun. He shakes his head, knocking the thought from his mind. "I'm sorry," Taurin says, his voice strained. "I've spent over a day in the desert with little food or drink, and I'm jumpy. It won't happen again."

Claw pulls the blade away from Taurin's shirt and rests his arm at his side. "It is not just the lack of nourishment that causes your blood to boil, boy. It's the flecks in your eyes and the power that surges inside you like an untamed bolt of lightning. You have to learn to control it, or it will end you."

"You can help me with that?"

"Perhaps, but first I need something from you."

Taurin swallows hard. The thought of what a man like Claw could want from him makes his body shiver and his blood run cold. "What do you need me to do?"

"Good boy." Claw grabs a large roll of parchment on the desktop and unrolls it on the flat surface. Yellowed from age and scarred with a dozen burn marks, it looks to be much older than anything else in the room. "Do you know what this is?"

Taurin leans in and examines the ancient paper. Hundreds of black lines connect to make square rooms paired with wide doorways and long, winding hallways. "Is this some kind of building diagram?"

"It is," Claw says, his voice guarded. "Have you seen such a thing before?"

"Not exactly, but I've studied a few books about engines and machines. They all have drawings like this."

"Excellent. Do you understand what each of the markings mean and know how to translate them?"

Taurin shakes his head. "I know how to read a diagram, but I've never seen anything like this before. It doesn't even look like a real building. Seems fake."

"That is because few have ever seen it, and those who have either will not or cannot speak."

"The Watch Force compound?"

"Yes. What you see before you has cost me more than you can imagine." Claw steps back and motions for Taurin to come closer to the diagram. "Please, study it with care."

Taurin spends several minutes looking over every line and symbol that covers the faded parchment, but it's no use. "So, where is it?" Taurin asks, frustrated. "I don't see anything on here that shows where to find the compound."

"That's where I need your help," Claw explains.

"How am I supposed to find a secret building that I didn't even know existed until a few days ago?"

"Oh, I have a feeling you will find it. With the help of your friends, of course."

A twinge of guilt stabs at Taurin's chest. He'd forgotten, for a while, about Violet and Shrift. Claw's actions had stolen his attention. They could be in serious danger, and he didn't even think to ask. "Are they safe? Can I see them?"

"Your friends are fine, no thanks to you." Claw smiles. "A little sore, perhaps, but nothing that can't be mended."

Taurin's face flashes red with anger. "Can I see them?"

"In time, but first you must agree to my terms."

"What terms?"

Claw pulls another cigar from his pocket and slices its tip with his blade. A blue flame leaps from his hand and lights the rolled tobacco. Puffs of gray smoke float into the air once more, covering the bald man's face before they dissipate. Finally, he speaks. "A man called the Seer is using the Watch Force to hunt, gather, and kill all those he suspects are Organics. This has been going on for years, but his efforts have increased exponentially over the past few months. That is a problem for me."

"What's that have to do with me?" Taurin asks.

"Stop interrupting and *listen*!" Claw demands. Purple veins throb in his neck, and gray flecks, like hot ash from one of his cigars, shimmer in his eyes. "You must kill this man before he finds me and robs me of everything I have made. He *must* be stopped!

The request hits Taurin like a hammer to the skull. Even with all his influence and might, Claw still fears the Seer and his army of suited patrolmen. What then could a boy like him do against such a powerful adversary? Tears form in Taurin's eyes, and one trickles down his cheek before he can stop it. Pulp and Cay will be lost, and there is nothing he can do about it—perhaps there never was. "I can't help you," Taurin says, holding back a river of tears. "It's over."

Claw steps close to Taurin, his face tight like leather. "It isn't over until I say it is."

"What can I do that you can't?"

"Find the Seer and kill him. Those are my terms."

"But I—"

"Either do what I ask, or you and your friends die tonight. You have five seconds to decide. It makes no difference to me."

Taurin rubs his tired eyes with blood-spattered hands. Agreeing to Claw's demands will only delay the inevitable, but it's the only choice he has that keeps everyone alive for another day. "I'll do it."

"Of course you will. The Seer is a menace and needs to be eliminated. Take the diagram and get out of my face before I change my mind."

Taurin grabs the parchment from the desk and twists it into a tight roll. Without a word, he turns and follows the smeared blood on the floor to the door at the back of the room, hesitating before he opens it. *It would be easy to just kill Claw and never worry about him again.* The thought tortures his mind once more, but now isn't the time for vengeance. "Is someone going to slit my throat when I leave?"

Claw, who is now sitting on the front of his desk, shrugs. "You will have to open it and find out."

Taurin swings the door wide with a single, powerful shove and steps into a cramped room. The polished redwood floors in Claw's office are replaced here with crushed stone and packed dirt. Wide planks of warped, mismatched wood make up the walls, and rusted sheets of metal act as the ceiling. In the center of the room lies a girl's lifeless body.

"Violet!" Taurin shouts. He slips on the loose gravel as he rushes to his friend. He kneels beside her and brushes away long strands of tangled hair. Though bloody and bruised, Violet's face still glows with life. Shame fills his chest once more. Her bruises and spilled blood are because he wasn't being careful. He leans down and kisses her cheek. "I'm sorry."

"Well, ain't that a pretty sight." Shrift says, stepping out of the shadows. "Thought you were dead."

"Is she okay?" Taurin asks, ignoring Shrifts words. "I just found her like this."

"She ain't gonna win any beauty pageants tomorrow, but she'll be fine after a rest." Shrift walks over to Taurin and kneels next to Violet. "Partner, you should've seen her."

"What are you talking about?"

"They were rough on her, with fists and such, but she didn't give 'em the satisfaction of knowing they were hurting her. Stood and took every hit. Never said a word."

Taurin looks down at Violet. "She's always been tougher than me. Even when we were young. I'd fall and cry. She'd fall, get up, and just keep running."

Shrift squeezes Taurin's shoulder. "She'll get back up and keep kicking your ass tomorrow. Trust me."

"I know." Taurin wipes his eyes with the back of his hand. A smear of red marks his face where fresh tears mix with dried blood. "I should have been here."

"Why's that?" Shrift pulls his hand away. "So you could get your face beat in and have matching bruises?"

"No, I could have stopped them."

"Listen here, little man. Don't take away from what she did tonight by sayin' you coulda done it better. That ain't fair and you know it. Hopefully her pain was worth something."

"Here," Taurin says, handing Shrift the rolled parchment.

"What is it?"

"You tell me."

Shrift lays the diagram on the ground and opens it, studying it with his blue eyes. "I know this place," he finally says. "This is where those bastards kept me."

"It's the Watch Force compound. At least, that's what Claw told me. I needed to hear the same from you."

"If Pulp and Cay are anywhere, they are here." Shrift points a gloved finger to a small circle drawn in the center of the page. "This is where they tried to hold me."

Taurin nods. "All I know is that we are running out of time. We need to get going."

"You're forgettin' a promise you made to me. I can't leave this town without paying my debt. You race for me tomorrow, and I take you to this hell hole." Shrift gestures toward the paper. "That's our deal."

"Can't you see that things have changed?" Taurin asks, frustration coating his words. "Claw said he'd kill us if we don't leave. Staying isn't possible."

"He'll kill me if he finds out I was here and didn't pay up. Then your fancy drawing of a building will be useless."

"You're telling me that you owe your debt to Claw?"

Shrift flashes Taurin a wide smile. "Yeah, and as you found out, he isn't the most forgiving of fellas. So, you better be as good at racin' as this pretty little lady said you were."

"Just pick her up, and let's get out of here."

"I know just the place to crash for the night," Shrift says.

CHAPTER 18: CAVE

HOT LIQUID splatters against Taurin's face, waking him from an otherwise restful night's sleep. The bitter taste on his lips and the acidic smell in his nose are hard to place at first, but then he opens his groggy eyes and sees the source of the liquid. A mangy gray goat stands just inches from his face, and a pungent, steady stream of urine pours from the animal, spilling on Taurin's cheeks. "Yuck!" Taurin leaps from the ground and wipes the remaining fluid off his face and lips. "That's disgusting."

"Don't scare him." Shrift says from across the room. "He's a little jumpy."

"What does he have to be scared of?"

"Of this, I'd guess." Shrift plunges the silver tip of his blade into the goat's neck, severing the animal's jugular vein and spilling a river of crimson on the ground. One moment the animal is alive and the next it isn't, lying unmoving against a pile of rotting hay.

Shocked and still a bit sleepy, Taurin watches in silence. He has no words; just a soft moan ekes out of his throat. Fresh blood pours from the goat's wound and colors the once-yellow hay a murky brown. The animal's lifeless eyes stare up at him. Its dark, pink tongue dangles from its mouth.

"What?" Shrift asks. "Never seen blood before?"

"Of course I have, but you could have warned me first."

"Where's the fun in that?" Shrift skins the goat quickly and removes all the unwanted bits from the animal. The process takes just a few minutes, and then only slabs of raw, pink meat wrapped in cream-colored fat remain. "If you're done being useless, I could use a hand."

"Sure," Taurin says, fumbling for words. It didn't even cross his mind to help with cleaning the goat. The process was mesmerizing to watch. He'd helped prepare animals before, but the way Shrift did it was almost magical. He gave each movement such care and focus that Taurin could do little but stare.

"We need a fire so we can cook the meat. I bet even you can handle that." Shrift points to a pile of twigs and branches he gathered.

"How am I supposed to do that? Do you have matches?"

A look of utter annoyance covers Shrift's face, and he frowns. "Seriously?"

Of course, Taurin thinks. He moves to the pile of gathered timber, focusing on the twigs. The flecks of crimson shimmer in his eyes as an image of a single blue flame, hot and wild, flickers in his mind. He holds a steady hand over the wood, and within seconds, the kindling crackles with orange fire. Taurin grins with confidence. Pulling fire from his mind isn't a new skill, but to call it with such ease feels amazing.

"Don't get too cocky," Shrift says. "Telling wood to burn is like telling a fish to swim. It's natural." He holds a slender metal spike, covered from end to end with raw goat meat, over the center of the fire. The meat crackles and steams from the heat. The scent of smoke and char waft through the air, causing Taurin's stomach to rumble.

Hunger hasn't been much of a concern for Taurin on this journey. True, he's noticed the pain in his gut at times, and he's enjoyed food when Violet reminds him to eat something, but otherwise it's seemed unimportant. Pushing forward into the Wasteland, finding Pulp, and making someone accountable for his father's death have been all that mattered. Now, looking at the pink meat roasting in the open flames, his mouth waters with anticipation.

"Smells good. Doesn't it, Violet?" When she doesn't respond, he looks behind him and then to each of his sides. To his dismay, Violet is missing. "Violet?"

"Ain't here," Shrift replies while tending to the goat. "Gone before I woke up."

"Where is she?"

"If I knew that, I'd a done told you."

"She could be hurt or taken or—"

"Or right behind you," Violet interrupts. A pile of split wood fills her arms, and a cloth bag of produce hangs from her left shoulder.

"Where have you been?" Taurin yells, his voice hard. "We thought they took you!"

"We didn't think anything of the sort," Shrift says. "Loverboy was worried."

"Can you blame me?" Taurin glares at Shrift. "Feels like every time I close my eyes, something terrible happens. Sorry if being tired of people dying bothers you."

"Relax," Violet says, her voice calm and soft. "I couldn't sleep, so I went exploring for a bit. Nothing happened. Harbor Town really is not such a bad place."

"Not such a bad place?" Taurin repeats. "You mean besides the gang of thugs that mangled your face?" Even before the words leave his lips he knows they aren't right, but he can't stop them from spewing from his mouth.

Violet reaches up to feel her swollen cheeks, then presses her fingertips against her split, blood-stained lips. The thugs' fists had been hard against her skin, but their words were what stung the most. Two men, each marked with Claw's signature—three claw slashes tattooed just below their left eyes—spit insults and phrases at her that she'd never heard before, each more ugly and foul than the last. They wanted her to tell them about Taurin and his abilities, but she didn't say a word. She met all their demands with silence.

"I'm sorry," Taurin says. "I didn't mean to say that."

"You can be such a baby," Violet responds. "You were still sleeping, so I didn't wake you. I figured you'd need your rest for the race, and maybe one of these." She throws a bright-red apple at Taurin's chest. "I know it's your favorite."

Taurin instinctively snatches the apple before it hits the ground and holds in it his hands, staring at its red skin and examining the peel's firmness like a treasure. He licks his lips and groans at the thought of the apple's sweet juice on his tongue.

"Gonna kiss it or eat it?" Shrift says, shaking his head. "You sure are a strange bird."

Taurin sinks his teeth into the apple's skin, drowning out Shrift's insult with the sound of the fruit's crunchy flesh. Crisp, sweet flavors explode in his mouth as he devours every inch of the apple, gnawing it down to just the core and a few black seeds in a matter of seconds. He closes his eyes, lost in the pleasure of the delicacy, and breathes deeply. "Thank you," Taurin finally says, looking at Violet. "I didn't know how much I needed that."

"I did." Violet leans over until her face is just inches from Taurin's. Her lips part from a moment, as if preparing for a kiss, but instead she moves her hand to Taurin's lips and wipes away a smear of apple residue. "Got it." Then she turns back to her cloth sack and pours the contents onto the wooden floor. Three potatoes, two long carrots, and a handful of red berries spill out in front of her. "It isn't much, but I didn't have a lot to trade."

"It's more than enough," Shrift says. "I can cook these right up with the goat, if you'd like."

"Perfect." Violet leans over and kisses Shrift on the forehead. "Handy to have a cook around."

Shrift's neck flushes with crimson. "Ain't no trouble. Just wish I had some salt or spice to liven it up a bit. Might be a little bland."

Three loud booms shake the room's wooden door. Startled, Taurin stands and steps in front of Violet. "Did anyone follow you here?"

"I'm not sure," Violet whispers.

Shrift reaches to his side and pulls his copper heat pistol from its holster. He silently steps past his companions and to the doorway. *Bam. Bam. Bam.* Three more knocks hammer against the door. "Who's there?" Shrift yells. "Whatcha want with us?"

"It's me," a gruff voice mutters from behind the door. "The girl told me to find you here."

Without further discussion, Violet walks past Shrift and pulls the door open. The bright morning sun shines high behind a short, fat man balancing a gleaming ash speeder upright against his side. "Oh, I forgot I ran into Rolff while I was out." She smiles. "Come inside. I'm glad you made it."

"At least someone is," Rolff says, squinting at Shrift. "Wasn't sure if the lot of you were still alive until I saw this girl's beautiful face wandering around this morning. Lucky I found her before someone else did."

"Yeah, real lucky," Shrift says. "Guess you had nothin' to do with us getting clubbed in the head and dragged into Claw's place last night, huh? Guess that was just a weird coincidence?"

"I knew nothing about that. I swear!" Rolff scoots back to the door, sliding his steps against the floor. "I barely got away myself, and good thing I did!"

"Why is that a good thing? Seems to me a knock to the face would do your fat head some good," Shrift growls. His blue eyes flash white for a moment, and he clenches his fists. "Maybe I should be the one to deliver it."

"No, no!" Rolff pleads. "You have it all wrong. I'm your friend. Look and see what I brought you." He runs his round fingers over the side of the speeder. The black paint that once covered the machine has been replaced with a deep red that sparkles in the sunlight. "Isn't she beautiful? I worked all night getting it ready to race."

Shrift pushes past Rolff's round belly and places his hand on the speeder, tracing the lines of the frame. "The paint sucks, but the rest seems to check out."

"Let me see," Taurin says, walking over to the machine. He studies the speeder and tests each wire and hose. Then he kneels next to the engine, pulls the dipstick free, and examines the thick black liquid that coats it. "He's actually done a nice job with it."

"I told you," Rolff responds. "The boy likes it, as I said he would. Now do you believe your old friend?"

Shrift shrugs in response, then turns and walks back to the crackling fire. He twists the spike holding the cooking meat in the same way Taurin tested the speeder: with steady and skilled movements. "Someone hand me that," he says, gesturing to a cast-iron pot near the edge of the fire. "It's filled with water, so be careful."

Violet picks up the pot and walks it over to the fire, careful not to spill a drop of water. The fire reflects red light on the side of Shrift's face; the white flecks in his eyes are muted now. "Here you go," she says. "I didn't realize you had something to cook in."

"Tough to know anything when you leave without saying nothing to no one." Shrift grabs the pot and nestles it into the flames. First, he slices the potatoes and the carrots with his knife. Then, he tosses them into the warming water. Within seconds, the water hisses to life. Steam crawls toward the ceiling as the fresh vegetables boil. "Least you had sense to bring back food. Can't imagine what you had to give up for these."

"Just a few things in the satchel my father gave Taurin and me. A few oddities that a local merchant liked well enough to trade."

"Not the tablet," Taurin blurts. "You didn't trade that, did you? We still need it."

"Tablet?" Rolff, his eyebrows rising high on his face, asks. "What is the boy talking about, my dear?"

"Nothing," Violet responds. "He just woke up and is confused. Father gave us a book of bound pages he called his tablet. Nothing more than a few scribbles and markings."

"Right," Taurin adds. "Had a map of the area, and I didn't want to lose it. No big deal, really."

The fat man studies Taurin's face, watching for any clues or signs of deceit.

"How 'bout you all shut your mouths and come get some of this meal before it gets cold? Didn't bust my ass making it so it could go to waste," Shrift says. "So, Rolff, get your pig-face over here and stop hasslin' that kid. I done told you he ain't nothing to no one."

"Fine," Rolff growls. "But if I find you're keeping something from me, I'll …"

"You'll what?" Taurin asks, towering above Rolff, his eyes hot with fire. "My friend here is offering you a meal. Take it or get out. Either way, I couldn't care less." He brushes past the fat man and sits down next to the fire. Everyone in the room falls silent. The phrase, bold and threatening, isn't like Taurin—or, at least, the Taurin who first started this journey.

"You're learnin' after all," Shrift says, a wide smile covering his face. "Glad to see you growing a backbone."

"Getting tired of being pushed around," Taurin says.

Violet sits down next to Taurin and lays her hand on his leg. "Save your anger for the race. The merchant I traded with told me it can be rough. You'll need to race dirty."

Taurin reaches into the flames and rips a hunk of cooked goat meat from the metal spike. His skin sizzles as the fire dances on his fingers before he tosses the pink scrap in his mouth. "That won't be a problem," Taurin mumbles between chews. "I'm ready to make someone else hurt."

CHAPTER 19: INTRODUCTIONS

PILES of split rock and ground minerals line the edge of the sea wall next to the processing plant. The abandoned, crumbling factory stands as a reminder only of what was once here, rather than what remains. For years, the people of Cinder came to this place to dig and crush the mountains in order to unleash a hidden power in red stones. Untamed volcanoes once pumped hot, boiling liquid down the sides of the onyx rocks that surround the area. That fusion of fire and black stone created a power source that once fueled everything in Cinder—fire crystals.

The brick chimneys that tower above the factory once pumped plumes of thick gray smoke into the sky as the people of Cinder slaved inside the processing plant. Fire crystals were worth far more to those who desired them than the lives of the people who dug the red jewels from the ground. Now, just the shadows of the dead and the haze from the years of smog remain. With the crystals long gone, the ash speeders gathered for the race are the only things of value in this place. All five sit idle at the starting line, waiting for the race to begin.

Taurin rests on top of his bright-red machine. He sits, quiet and patient, waiting for a man in a long black coat to finish inspecting the rest of the speeders and their racers. Taurin sits in the center of the five machines. Each rider, though different, looks ready to race, and perhaps to fight.

His mind is fixed on one thought—winning, at any cost. The coins from his victory would fund the rest of his journey; Shrift promised as much. Now, looking at the participants, his previous confidence wanes a bit. The other four racers have serious machines. True, his speeder is well equipped, but he didn't expect such competition. *Too late to turn back.*

"SILENCE!" A booming voice shouts.

Sweat drips down Taurin's neck, wetting the thin cotton shirt that covers his back. The man in front of the racers is both familiar and terrifying: Claw. His small stature is no match for his massive voice and commanding presence.

"These races are important," Claw says. "They prove those who can survive and those who cannot."

The racers and gathered spectators are silent as Claw speaks. Each eye is fixed on the bald man at the center of the dirt track; every ear is locked to his words as if they held the key to life and death. From the sound of his voice and the fierce look on his face, perhaps they do.

"Tonight, things are different." Claw pauses for a moment, his eyes locked on Taurin. "Tonight, the winner will only receive the prize if all other racers are eliminated." A soft rumble of excitement rolls through the crowd. Each of the five racers shuffles on his or her seat, anxious.

"To the death?" one of the spectators shouts.

"Only one survivor?" another asks.

"All but the champion must be dead by the end of the race, or no prize money will be given," Claw says. "If any more than one survives, then all who remain will be executed at the finish." A group of six armed men form a straight line behind Claw. Each take aim with their heat rifles at the racers. "With one word, I can end you now and save the trouble of a race. Do any wish such a fate?"

For a moment, not much longer than a breath, Taurin considers raising his hand. The burn of a heat rifle blazing a hole through his scalp would end this long journey and stop the pressure that pulses in his head. In a morbid way, it would be the ultimate relief. Everyone is counting on him to succeed: Pulp, Violet, Cay, Shrift, and even his father. They all expect greatness from him, but in his heart he knows he isn't special.

He's just a boy who's in over his head. The pressure to be something he's not is excruciating.

"I'll take your silence as an agreement to the terms," Claw continues. "Now then, let's meet our competitors!" A flurry of cheers and applause rises from the crowd. The bald man walks to the rider on Taurin's far left. Tattoos mark every inch of the girl's body that isn't covered by her leather racing jacket and matching black jeans. Wild strands of purple and pink hair fray against her back like stretched fireworks. White-framed goggles, paired with metallic lenses, fit tight against her narrow face. The reflective lenses protect her eyes, but her head is exposed: she wears no helmet. She rides a purple speeder that matches her hair. "This wisp of a girl is called Frawn. She may be young and look a bit frail, but don't let that fool you. I've seen her slit a man's throat just for holding his gaze a bit too long!"

A roar of laughter rolls from the crowd. Taurin realizes that this is just the kind of thing they've come to see—death. Everyone loves an underdog, especially one who isn't afraid to kill.

Claw makes his way to the next racer in line. Long gray hair, pulled back into a matted ponytail, streams down the old man's crooked back. His skin, dark like the onyx-colored mountains that surround the area, flaps loose against his frail bones. "This man needs no introduction for you who are fans of the racers, but still, his legend needs to be celebrated." Claw uses exaggerated arm movements and flamboyant language to address the crowd, whipping them into a frenzy like a ring leader exciting a circus audience. "This man is known by several names around our land, but today let's call him by his given name: Bowd!"

"Who let that old bag of bones in here?" a thin man with fewer teeth than fingers shouts from the stands. A mix of cheers and boos ring out from the crowd.

"This old man is the most successful racer ever to compete in the ash races. I know that vexes some of you gathered here," Claw continues. "He has killed a few of your friends and some of your family, no doubt, but today may be the day he pays the price for those past victories!"

Bowd stays silent. His speeder is made from silver sheets of metal hand-fitted on a simple gray frame. It, like its rider, is seasoned and shows signs of a full life: gashes, dents, and scuffs mark its metal. Taurin looks the speeder over from a distance. It's battered, but from what he can tell, the machine can still go fast—he knows that with a racer like Bowd driving it anything is possible.

Claw walks past Taurin, skipping his introduction, and instead pounds his fist against the bare chest of a massive man seated on an equally bulky ash speeder. The giant's skin ripples with muscle. A white tattoo of three slash marks colors the left side of his face. Skill and experience matter little when you're one of Claw's men.

"A race wouldn't be complete without one of my handpicked hit men. He's here to make sure the others follow the rules." Claw shoots an angry look in Taurin's direction. This speech is for him, Taurin realizes. Claw is making sure Taurin knows that someone is watching—always. "Sarzz is his name, though what he is called does not matter. He represents me on the track tonight. If he wins, then I win. If I win, then …" Claw pauses and looks to the crowd with wide, wild eyes. "WE ALL WIN!"

Cheers roar from the crowd, shaking the ground beneath the ash speeders' tires. The bald man reaches into a leather pouch tied to his side and throws a handful of gold coins into the air over the crowd. An explosion of violence breaks out in the stands. Bones crack and snap as the spectators fight for the coins. An old woman, her back arched and hands thin like glass, is crushed beneath the spectators' heavy feet. No one extends a hand to help her off the dirt—the gold sparkles too brightly for anyone to consider what it costs.

"Silence!" Claw shouts, and in an instant the wild crowd calms. Everyone turns, their mouths closed tightly, and watches him walk to the next racer.

A boy, younger than Taurin by at least three years, sits on an oversized speeder. His jacket hangs awkwardly on his narrow shoulders like a bed sheet on a meager tree branch. The boy's brown hair is buzzed short on his head; his brown eyes are burrowed deep in his anemic face just above his sharp cheekbones. He wipes the sweat pouring from his forehead with a shaking hand that looks like mere bone and skin, but it's a useless gesture. The boy is terrified and everyone can see it.

"Pity," Claw says. "Such a young boy is forced to pay the debt of his useless father. The coward took his life rather than pay what was owed to me, and now his son must try his luck at this race to make things even." Claw pats the boy's face gently. "It's a bit sad, but as we all know here in Harbor Town, a debt must be paid …" Claw pauses and cups his hand around his ear.

"NO MATTER THE COST!" the crowd roars in unison.

"No matter the cost," Claw repeats and walks toward the crowd. Taurin spots Shrift standing in the front, his thick arms cross against his chest. White flecks cloud his eyes, lightening an otherwise shadowed face. Claw spots Shrift too, and locks his eyes on Taurin's companion. "Are you ready?" Claw asks the crowd, though he continues to watch Shrift as he speaks.

The crowd shouts, "LET IT BEGIN!"

"Yes, let it begin," Claw repeats. He nods to Shrift, whose eyes still shine bright with rage, and walks back to the starting line.

"I should just kill him and be done with this." Shrift spits a glob of saliva onto the sand.

"Relax," Violet whispers, her voice calm and focused. "You aren't alone anymore." She places her hand on Shrift's arm. "Trust that Taurin will take care of everything."

"Why should I?"

"Because you know it's true." She pulls her hand away and runs her fingers through the wild strands of dark hair that the wind keeps blowing in her face. "This isn't your fight."

Shrift looks over at Taurin seated on the red speeder. He looks confident—ready. Violet knows she is right. There's nothing she or Shrift can do to help Taurin.

"It's always my fight," Shrift mumbles.

"What is your name?" Claw asks the young boy at the starting line.

"Redge," the boy mumbles, his voice shaking.

"Speak up, boy!" Claw yells. "I need to know what name to put on your tombstone!" The crowd roars with laughter again.

"Redge!" the boy yells, tears streaming down his narrow face. "My name is Redge!" Claw reaches for the silver helmet hanging from the handlebars on Redge's speeder and slides in onto the boy's head. It, too, is oversized, meant for a larger man, and sits loose on his head. The clear visor does little to hide Redge's embarrassment or his tears. The boy shakes visibly, and a stream of yellow liquid spills down his pants and pools in the sand below his speeder.

"Finally," Claw says, moving to stand in front of Taurin, "we have a very special racer with us tonight. He comes from far beyond our walls and past the Wasteland to compete in our humble race. He boasts that he is the only *true* racer here tonight, so I think it's time Harbor Town proves him wrong!"

"Kill him now!" one voice shouts through the countless boos and cries from the crowd. Each cry is angrier than the last.

Claw leans into Taurin and whispers in his ear. "If you lose tonight, you're of no use to me. So, if you die, then so do your friends."

Taurin's heart beats so hard in his chest that it feels as though it may split him in half. Breathe, he tells himself. He sets his helmet on his head and slides the dark visor down, covering his face. Red flecks scorch his eyes, sending waves of fire through his body. The crowd can't be allowed to see his eyes burn. They'd turn him in to the Watch Force without a second thought. No, this race will need to be won with skill—not tricks or powers.

"Let's hear it for the *golden boy*!" Claw shouts. The crowd continues to boo, their rage so palpable that Taurin can almost feel it in the air.

"Riders, ready your machines!" Claw commands. "Remember the only rule is, *survive*!"

CHAPTER 20: THE RACE

MOUNTAINS the color of thick, crude oil mark the start of a winding ten-mile path. The race surface is a mixture of dirt, stone, and sand, and it's infused with a lethal blend of chemicals left over from decades of mining the fire crystals. Rusted barrels, oozing with toxic slime, are littered throughout the miles of rough roadway. Years ago when the crystals ran out and the factory closed, no one thought to clean up when they left. Now, Harbor Town claims the rusted wreckage and poisonous ponds as its own. This track is a slice of freedom for the hundreds gathered to watch the race—no matter how rotted and forgotten it seems.

Taurin's bare hands clench and unclench the hard rubber grips that coat his speeder's handlebars. This place is not where he should be right now. Pulp was taken and chained to a concrete wall and needs help—his help. In the beginning, he knew it wouldn't be easy, but the journey has turned out to be more difficult than he ever imagined. Each step has been harder than the last. Every choice brings with it a greater consequence than the last. Now he sits on top of a growling machine, waiting to begin a race that will most likely be his last.

Too late to run. Nowhere to hide. Just breathe.

Through the dark visor that covers his face, Taurin scans the crowd. Shrift's massive frame is easy to spot. He looks ready to strangle every person around him. Taurin almost wishes he would. It would make his night easier. Then he spots Violet. Her hair has been pulled tight behind her head in a ponytail-she was tired of the wind twisting it in front of her face. As if sensing him watching her, Violet stares back at him with intense eyes. She gives him a slight nod and an over-the-top thumbs-up gesture to show Taurin that she believes in him. For a moment, the tension in his mind relents and he allows himself to smile. How long ago was it that her lips almost found his in that dark forest? That was special, important. He nods, acknowledging his friend.

BLAM! BLAM! BLAM! Three shots ring out like explosions. The five speeders kick sand into the air and smoke spills from their exhaust pipes as the racers accelerate away from the starting line. The race has begun, and the crowd screams with excitement. Claw makes his way through the frothing sea of people, surrounded by the safety of six armed guards. Steady and calm, he climbs a set of winding stairs to an elevated seating area perched above the finish line.

Violet shuffles closer to Shrift. "This is crazy," she shouts as Claw's men begin to dispense the many powders and pills the crowd craves. "You didn't say it would be like this."

"It's worse than I remember," Shrift says. He straightens his back and flexes his chest muscles as he scans the area. "Stay close. This crowd looks like it could get violent at any moment. But don't worry, I'll protect ya." He squeezes Violet's shoulder.

"I can handle myself," Violet snaps, brushing Shrift's hand away.

"Sorry, I just …"

"We shouldn't be here, but we are because of you. So just stand there, flex your muscles, and hope Taurin wins."

Just over a mile away from the starting line, red flecks sparkle in Taurin's eyes. The speed is intoxicating, and he pushes his machine faster with each passing second. A part of him knows that this is what he was made for. Had the Watch Force not taken so much, maybe he would have been a great racer. That would have made his father proud. He'd been the one to teach Taurin how to piece scraps of metal and wires together to create a working speeder. In truth, the junk speeders Taurin and his father had built behind their home failed more often than they ran, but that never mattered to Taurin. Oil and grit had seeped into his blood, and he'd fallen in love with the grime.

The fine-tuned machine that Taurin rides today is a far cry from the scrappers he used to race through the forest back home. This one was built for one thing: speed. *The Watch Force must need to be fast when they snatch children from their homes and murder innocent people,* he thinks. The thought breaks Taurin's joy like glass. He tightens his grip on the throttle and lowers his head. "Let's see what you can do."

Taurin watches as the air twists and flops Bowd's gray ponytail as he pulls up behind him. It hangs loose out the back of his helmet like a matted rope. He saw the old man race once before, though Bowd wouldn't recognize him. Taurin was just a kid in the crowd. He recognizes that the same meticulously maintained and hand-crafted ash speeder that Bowd used to win that race is the one that sits under him now. He sees the old man pat his speeder.

"Be a good girl," Bowd says. "Don't let me down."

Through the dust Taurin sees Sarzz just a few yards ahead of Bowd. He crouches over his speeder like a bear on a fat log. Sarzz turns his thick neck and shouts, "Time for some fun!"

Then, he releases his throttle, and brings his ash speeder to a dead stop in the center of the road.

Bowd's speeder spins its tires in front of Taurin. Sand and rock fly everywhere. Taurin steadies his speeder in time to watch the old man dodge a massive stone and speed around Sarzz by the slimmest of margins. Taurin's heart thumps in his chest and adrenaline throbs in his veins. *Too close*, he thinks. Then, he looks ahead and the world slows for a moment. A solid wall of stone stands tall, unmoving in front of Bowd. There is nothing he can do to help. It's too late.

Bowd slams into the mountain with such force it shakes sheets of rock and clouds of dark dust loose. Taurin turns his head as a burst of fire explodes from the wreckage. In an instant, Bowd's hand-forged speeder becomes a hurricane of deadly shrapnel. Taurin slams his brakes, bringing his speeder to a stop. Molten scraps of metal buzz past his helmet and dark smoke from the burning fuel surrounds him.

"Ha, ha," Sarzz's voice booms through the air. "Can't race a mountain."

Hidden, Taurin watches Sarzz approach the burning pile of rubble and step off his speeder. *What's he looking for?* Taurin wonders. *Bowd is dead*. Then, the smoke clears and he can see a hand reach for Sarzz's leg.

"Help me," Bowd screams. "Please."

A thick lump forms in Taurin's throat as he watches Sarzz shake the old man's hand from his leg, lift his boot, and slam it down against Bowd's head. The sound, like a block of ice being hit with a sledge hammer, makes Taurin sick and he has to fight not to retch.

"Claw, be proud!" Sarzz screams.

It takes just a few seconds for Sarzz to mount his powerful machine, its tires still damp with blood, and speed away. Taurin sits on his idling speeder and rubs his eyes. Guilt and anger fight in his mind. *You should have done something,* he thinks. The thought only lingers for a moment before Redge's roaring speeder drowns it out and reminds him there is still a race to win. Taurin twists his speeder's throttle, lowers his helmet, and speeds down the track.

Taurin moves his eyes right, then left, and then right again, tracking Redge's every movement. It takes time to make a pass on such a narrow path. Each side of the gravel road is covered with rusted barrels, boulders, and other hazards. He doesn't wish to end his race by being impatient. It's not that he couldn't cause Redge to make a mistake and crash, but Taurin made up his mind that he wouldn't take anyone's life—at least, not on purpose. There will be plenty of opportunity for racers to take themselves out of the competition.

A scattered line of metal barrels, each scarred with rusted holes and seeping noxious chemicals, sits idle in the middle of the track. Taurin sees the obstacles and makes a plan of attack. It would be easy if he were alone. He's made his way through much worse, but the unskilled racer ahead of him will complicate the maneuver. He watches Redge lean too far right to miss the first barrel and then make a frantic turn to the left to miss the second. *Sloppy*, Taurin thinks. Then, almost on cue, Redge's tires slip on a patch of wet sand and his heavy machine hammers into the third barrel. His thin arms pull hard against the handlebars and, to Taurin's surprise, the young boy steadies his speeder and rushes ahead. Shaking his head in annoyance, Taurin opens his throttle. Waiting has cost him time, and he needs to make it up.

A dark, deep canyon weaves along the right side of the roadway. With the mountains casting their long shadows over the opening, it's rare to see the bottom of the gorge during the day. It's impossible to see after the sun sets. Taurin watches Redge's headlight flicker as his tires bounce against rough rocks. The boy turns his head to look behind him.

"Watch out!" Taurin screams, but his voice is muted by the noise of the dueling engines. His hands tremble and the flecks burn brightly in his eyes. It was a mistake for the boy to take his focus off the road, but it's too late now. Taurin watches the beast of a machine pull the small boy to the ground. Sand and rock spray like bullets as the ash speeder drags Redge toward the canyon. Without thinking, Taurin leaps from his speeder and slides face-first across the gravel. Rocks rip his clothes and tear his skin, but his hand still finds what it was searching for. "I've got you," Taurin grunts, grabbing the boy's hand. He watches the boy's speeder fall into the darkness below him. The canyon swallowed the machine whole, and it would have done the same to Redge if Taurin hadn't grabbed his hand.

"Who are you?" Redge asks. The sloppy helmet that bobbled on his head fell off during the crash. Blood pours down the front of his face and trickles against his split lips.

"Taurin, and I've got you."

"I'm Redge."

"I know. Just grab my arm with your other hand, and I'll pull you out of here."

"That was my dad's. He loved it."

"Redge, I don't have time for this." Taurin squeezes the young boy's hand harder. The weight of his oversized gear is pulling the boy down and making his gloved-hands hard to grip. "Take my hand."

Dark-brown eyes stare up at Taurin. "You special, right? Eyes all sparkly like stars."

"Stop talking and give me your hand!"

"I wanted to be special. Do sumpin' to make my family proud. Haven't had no chances."

"Plenty of time still." Taurin's body slips and his free hand reaches for something solid, but he finds only loose sand and stones.

"Maybe for you. I'm just a nobody with no future."

"I'm slipping, so just grab my arm and I'll pull you up!"

Tears wet the small boy's cheeks. "Claw promised to take care of my family if I died. My turn to be special." Thin fingers twist and turn inside the oversized glove, and in a moment they are free.

"Redge!" Taurin watches the young boy float through the air and fall into the darkness below. His fingers still grip the empty leather glove. "I had you!" Taurin yells into the canyon. Then he drops his chin to his chest and shakes his head. It was easy to see himself in Redge, wanting to do more and be more for his family. "I had you." He smears tears off his cheeks with dirty hands.

Taurin's ash speeder lies on its side, the engine still purring in the sand. It feels like hours have passed, but in reality, it's been just a few minutes. *Still time. Keep moving. Pulp needs you*, he tells himself. With a single push, he straightens the machine and slings his leg over the side. He grips the handlebars with dirty, bloody knuckles, trying not to think about Redge. Grief will have to wait; there is still a race that needs to be won.

TAURIN

CHAPTER 21: MOUNTAINS

ONLY THREE racers remain: Taurin, Frawn, and Claw's henchman, Sarzz. Each push their speeders faster in an attempt to stay ahead, or, in Taurin's case, to catch up. Guilt still turns and twists inside his belly. The same thoughts echo in his mind, reminding him that someone else has slipped through his fingers: *I should have done more. I could have done more.*

Just ahead of Taurin, Frawn's metallic-purple ash speeder rockets down the track. Her machine is light and nimble, just like her. Vibrant tattoos of wild animals paint her skin. Each creature is more ferocious than the last. Strands of her purple and pink hair smack at the dark sky behind her. From the moment Claw's pistol fired, she was a blur. Until now.

Heavy clouds dim the moonlight and shrink Taurin's vision to just a few feet in front of his speeder. The Watch Force equipped the machine with a single headlight, which was perfect for weaving and winding through Cinder's narrow pathways. The small bulb's power is muted, however, by the endless sands that cover the Wasteland. A quick burst of light flashes ahead of him, and Taurin slows his red speeder to a stop. He slides his dark visor up with a flip of his wrist and stares into the darkness. "Hello?" he whispers. "Anyone—"

A hard thump on his head knocks Taurin from his machine and sends him crashing to the ground. Stars and lights spin in front of his eyes. For a few moments he lies dazed on the side of the road, unable to move. Then he sees her standing above him. Frawn's goggles no longer hide her secret: her eyes are lit with purple fire.

"You okay?" Frawn asks. "You took a big hit."

"I'm fine," Taurin responds, rubbing the growing lump on his forehead.

"Don't look it." She extends her slender hand, reaches down and takes hold of Taurin's wrist. "Let me help."

Taurin shoves her hand away. "No thanks." He knocks the dust off his jacket and pushes himself up from the ground. Frawn stands in front of him with her hands on her hips and her head tilted to one side. "Why did you hit me?" he asks.

"Needed you to stop."

"I was stopped. I saw your light."

"Hmm. Guess I just wanted to then." Frawn smiles, revealing two rows of uneven yellow teeth. If she ever cleaned them, it didn't show. "And I need you."

"For what?"

Frawn points a long black fingernail first to her left eye and then to her right. "These eyes brought me a lot of trouble that I need to leave behind. Think you might understand." She wiggles the same black nail in front of Taurin's eyes. "Flecks are dangerous."

For a second Taurin waits to answer. Part of him is thrilled to find someone else like him, and an equal part of him is cautious—even scared. "What do you want?" he asks.

"To be forgotten. To be dead."

"I'm not going to kill you!"

"Calm down, psycho. I just need to be fake dead." Frawn kneels down and draws a rough image of a bird in the sand with her fingernail. "I'm tired of running."

"I know the feeling." Taurin kneels next to the girl. Her bright tattoos, full of color, crawl up the sides of her neck like vines. Kneeling next to her, Taurin notices for the first time that her wrists are narrow and her cheeks are sunken in. It looks like she hasn't eaten in days. "How old are you?" he asks.

"Old enough to be on my own," Frawn says defensively. She stands and straightens her shoulders, dismissing the question. "You either help me or kill me. Your choice."

"I think enough people are out to kill people like us," he says. He stretches his hand to hers. "Help me up, and I'll do what I can."

Grinning, Frawn pulls Taurin from the dirt. "That idiot, Sarzz, will be here any second, and I've got a plan." She cups her hand and whispers into his ear, going over each step in detail.

"You can do that?" Taurin asks, his jaw hanging open in surprise.

"Yup. I'm a badass."

"If you say so." Taurin smiles.

"You can do all those things, right? I mean, you're *him*?"

"I'm me. Not sure if that's enough or not."

"Guess we're about to find out."

Taurin watches the sand swirl around the charging ash speeder. Sarzz keeps his head down in an attempt to block the debris, but from what Taurin can tell the flying rocks and grime still tear at the henchman's face. "I'm coming for you!" Sarzz growls.

"Get ready," Frawn commands. "He'll be here in a second, so don't screw this up."

Annoyed, Taurin responds, "Thanks for the support."

"Oh, grow up." Frawn raises her hands to the sky and curls her fingers into fists. Her eyes burn with purple heat, and an intense brightness spreads through her body, lighting each of her tattoos like neon. The inked animals crawl and prowl on her thin arms—alive. "Come to me!" she yells at the sky.

Taurin's crimson flecks throb in sequence with the quickening beat of his heart. The sight of Frawn's glowing body is something he never expected. She told him what would happen, yet seeing her tattoos move and twitch is unlike anything he could have imagined. Beads of sweat drip down Taurin's nose. His sand-covered fingertips sizzle and smoke. His crimson eyes search the sky, looking for help—nothing. "Anytime," Taurin says through clenched teeth.

"Time for fun," Sarzz croaks. "My speeder is hungry!"

Standing in the middle of the track, Taurin stretches his fingers wide and looks to the sky once more. In the distance he sees what he's been waiting for. "Finally."

"Swarm!" Frawn shrieks, and on command, hundreds of black birds dive toward Sarzz. Wild and ferocious, with wingspans as long as the girl is tall, the winged animals caw and scream as they approach their target.

"Stupid birds," Sarzz barks. He lowers his massive head until it rests behind the speeder's glass visor. "Stopping is death. Keep moving, keep pushing."

"He's not stopping," Taurin says, twisting his boots in the sand as he backs away from the roadway. "He was supposed to stop." He looks for Frawn, frantic. She should be easy to spot with wild animals glowing on her arms, but it's hard to see anything with a swarm of birds kicking up billows of dust.

Frawn grabs Taurin's shoulder and spins him to face her. "Didn't work. Time for a new plan."

"Think on the run!" Taurin grabs Frawn's hand, and they sprint toward a massive black mountain. At its base is a wide opening leading to a tunnel.

"Do you trust me?" Frawn asks.

The phrase rings familiar in Taurin's ears. It's the same thing he'd asked Violet before this trip began. She did then, so it's only fair to return the favor. "Sort of."

"Good enough!"

Black birds dive at Sarzz, their beaks ripping the flesh from his exposed arms and back. Blood covers his chest and face, but the birds do little to slow his momentum. "Takes more than birds!" Sarzz growls.

At the opening of the tunnel, Frawn and Taurin stop to catch their breath. It's time for a new plan.

"You've got this kind of magic, right?" Frawn asks, pointing to the mountain.

"I don't know. I think so."

"Thinking isn't enough. Can you do it?" She looks at Taurin, her purple eyes pleading. "This is my chance out."

Taurin shakes his head. "Come with me. I'll keep you safe."

"I don't need to be safe. I need to be free."

Sarzz hammers at the black birds with his fist, knocking several from the sky like paper. Fresh blood drips from his jaw, but his speeder roars ahead. To Taurin he looks wild, dangerous. "Still coming!" Sarzz yells.

"Fine, I'll do it," Taurin says. "But this kind of thing will wipe me out, so you can't leave me."

Frawn nods. "Wouldn't dream of it."

Taurin takes Frawn's hand and squeezes hard. "Promise me."

"Fine. I promise," Frawn says, shaking her hand free. "If you're done, I've got work to do." She runs to the tunnel's entrance and raises her hands in the air. "Push!" Her voice cracks with strain. Then, as if pulled by a giant rope, the crazed birds turn toward her.

"It's working," Taurin says, excited. He watches the flock spin Sarzz as they peck and scratch his eyes. Surely the henchman planned to stay on the dirt track and avoid the tunnel, but now he has no choice. Taurin looks toward Frawn and sees that she's still in battle with the sky. She pushes and moves the flock like a river, her arms stretched toward the birds. He's amazed and a bit terrified to watch her manipulate the animals with such ease.

Frawn turns her head suddenly and locks her purple eyes on him. "You going to stand there and stare or actually help?"

Taurin throws his hands up in surrender. "I'm on it." He grabs Frawn's hand and rushes out of the tunnel. The black cloud of birds pushes Sarzz toward the tunnel's opening, and Taurin sees that it's time. *Strong as stone. Crack like ice.* Another lesson from Clue. First, a rock and this phrase on his doorstep. Back then, they were only the words on a stone plate. The mountain is neither a stone nor a plate, and he knows what he must do goes far beyond any lessons he has learned.

"What are you waiting for?" Frawn asks, her face twisted and frantic. "It's now or never!"

Taurin clears his mind, pushing away his fear and calming his heartbeat, and spreads his fingers against the rock before him. "Strong as stone. Crack like ice." The crimson flecks flicker, then burn in his eyes. His arms and hands throb with untamed energy. "Strong as stone! Crack like ice!" The ground begins to shake, and a wide, crooked crack grows in the side of the mountain. Boulders crash and break around Taurin. Black dust blinds him.

Frawn sees the mountain split and throws her hands above her head once again. "Away!" she shouts, and on cue, the swarm turns and flies into the sky.

At first, a few black stones fall from above, and then the sides of the tunnel crumble around Sarzz, knocking him from his speeder. Taurin can almost feel the rocks shatter Sarzz's bones and split his skin. He has to look away. The belly of the mountain will be the henchman's tomb and he is the one who buried him.

CHAPTER 22: ESCAPE

THE MOUNTAIN rumbles and rattles beneath Taurin's aching hands. The tips of his fingers are split and bloody, and his palms are ragged and ripped. He squeezes his swollen eyelids together, trying to block out the throbbing pain inside his head, but it's no use. He knew it would take every scrap of his energy to bring down the tunnel walls, but he never expected that releasing that kind of power would take such a physical toll on his body.

"Just hold on," Frawn says, her voice at a distance. "I'm coming!"

He opens his eyes, which are still fogged with crimson, in an attempt to find the source of the voice. Smears of gray and blotches of black are all Taurin can see. *Help me*, he thinks. The words stay stuck in his mind, unable to escape his lips. His hands stay locked against the stone, unwilling to release it.

Frawn's fingers close around Taurin's wrists and pull them away from the mountain. "I've got you." She lays Taurin down on the roadway. "Nice work."

Colors sweep across Taurin's vision again, bringing Frawn to life in front on him. Her tattoos swirl and twist brightly on her arms and neck.

"Thanks," Taurin says.

"For what?"

"For staying."

Frawn runs her fingers through the purple and pink strands of her hair. A tight-lipped smile curls her lips. "Won't be for long. I have to be dead, remember?"

Taurin nods. "Yeah, but I'm not sure how. The whole knocking down a mountain thing kind of drained me."

"That was nothing." Frawn laughs. "Think you can stumble back onto that thing?" Her cracked black fingernail points toward Taurin's speeder.

"With some help, probably."

Without a word Frawn bends down and hooks her hands under Taurin's armpits. Like an ant, her size doesn't show her true strength. She pulls him to the edge of the speeder and tosses him over the seat, belly down. "Heavier than I thought. Smellier too." She waves her hand in front of her nose.

Taurin rolls his eyes. "Not a lot of time for showers lately. I've been kind of busy."

"Everyone stinks out here. It's gross."

"Okay, so what's the plan to get somewhere that doesn't smell so bad?"

"I've got it covered." Frawn looks up to the sky. "Think you can slide your legs over that thing and hold on?"

Taurin pushes himself up and swings his leg over the seat with as much energy as he can muster. "No problem," he lies. Each bone and inch of his skin protests with pain. "Now what?"

"We fly." She lifts her hands above her head and shouts, "Carry!" Instantly the air turns black with feathers and wings. Hundreds of dark birds swoop down from the sky again and grab Frawn's arms and Taurin's speeder. Within seconds, the two are high above the collapsed tunnel, soaring like one of the many birds that carry them.

Taurin grips the handlebars so tightly that his knuckles turn white. His body shakes, and his breath catches in his chest. The roadway below them is just a line in the sand now. He's never been so high before—it's dizzying.

"Amazing, right?" Frawn shouts over the flapping of the flock of birds. "I love it up here!"

Taurin nods, his movements slow. He can feel his stomach twist and turn. Bringing down the mountain drained his powers, and now the height is stealing what little control he has left over his body. Pointing his index finger, he signals *down*.

"Thanks again," Frawn yells, her lips spread in a wide smile. "Don't forget to tell them you killed me!" She frees an arm from the flock's grip and motions to the birds holding Taurin and his speeder. "Land!" The word booms across the sky, and once again the cloud of black feathers responds.

Fast and without much warning, Taurin and his speeder fall toward the ground. The flock still holds him tightly, but the rate of the descent curdles the contents of his stomach. *Just hold on*, he tells himself. Sand and dirt fly up around him as the birds drop the speeder onto the track. His back cracks and his fingers snap against the metal machine upon impact, though thankfully it doesn't pop the speeder's tires. "Ouch!" Taurin cries, but no one is close enough to hear. Frawn has vanished in her cloud of black birds, and Shrift and Violet still wait with the rest of the crowd at the finish line.

The swarm leaves as fast as they came, and only a few fallen feathers show they were ever there. Taurin, alone on the edge of Harbor Town, sits and stares ahead. The rusted refinery, the finish line, is just under a mile away, but it might as well be a thousand. His crimson flecks are dull in his eyes;

his fingertips are split and bloody. The energy of his youth has been replaced with a heaviness and a tired ache. "Don't quit," he says out loud. "Turn the key." With shaking fingers, he twists the key and the speeder rumbles back to life.

No obstacles stand between Taurin and the end of the race, but completing the entire race is a requirement. If no one crosses the finish line, then no one wins. That isn't an option. *Be brave*, he tells himself. He twists the throttle with bruised palms, and the machine lurches forward. His tires spin on loose rock, and a cloud of gray exhaust trails behind him. The finish line is drawing near.

"I see him!" Violet's voice cracks as she pushes her way through a thick mob of onlookers. "It's Taurin!"

Shrift shoves past the fevered crowd. They've grown wilder since the race began—more violent. He saw one man rip another's eye from his socket just because he stepped on his foot. Another stabbed a man for calling him a thief. Pills and powders never stopped flowing through the crowd, each frothing fan spending whatever coins they had to feel good for a moment. "Buncha dogs," Shrift spits.

"Over here." Violet motions to Shrift. "He's coming!"

Shrift finally frees himself from the mob and comes to stand next to Violet as they look down the track. In the distance he sees a cloud of dust and hears the grumble of an engine. "You sure that's our boy?"

Violet bites her lip. *Of course it's him*, she thinks. *Taurin is the best, and he'd do anything to prove it*. Still, her heart catches in her throat as she watches the slow-moving machine pull closer. She'd feel it if something had happened to him—surely.

The crowd is slow to notice the racer's approach, but it soon roars with excitement as the speeder draws closer. Men make their way through the mob, dispensing the last round of Claw's treats. Loud music still blares over the scattered speakers, shaking the ground with unrelenting noise.

"Are you ready for a fantastic finish?" Claw's voice echoes through the air. "I know I am!" The bald man makes his way down from his perch, his guards protecting his every step until he stands next to the finish line.

Taurin wills the speeder forward. The gathered spectators, wild and lurid, are just blurs and sounds around him. The engine muffles the announcer's words, and darkness dulls all color. One image, however, does grab his attention: a bald man standing close to the finish line. Claw. The thought of crashing his machine into the cruel man flickers in Taurin's mind. It would be satisfying for a moment, but in the end, it would be a waste. Instead, he stops his machine just past the finish line and pulls his helmet from his head.

The crowd erupts with a mix of boos and cheers. "Silence!" Claw growls. His guards blast half a dozen heat rifles into the air to hush the crowd. "It seems we have a winner." Claw makes his way to Taurin and pats the front tire of the speeder. "Anyone left?"

The question hangs in front of Taurin for what feels like hours. His words are slow and stick in his mouth like tar. "No," he whispers. "They're all dead."

Violet exchanges a worried look with Shrift. "Do you think he killed someone?" she asks.

Shrift looks down at her, his eyes soft. "He did what he needed to. No shame in that."

Violet nods. "No shame."

"Ha, ha! Wonderful," Claw laughs. "We knew you could do it. Didn't we?" He looks to the crowd and raises his arms to the sky. "DIDN'T WE?" The crowd cheers and claps on cue.

One man, his eyes wild from the pills and powders, shrieks, "He cheated! I know he—" A single blast from one of Claw's henchmen silences the protestor. His limp body collapses against the sand. No one else complains.

"Step down, boy; you are victorious!" Claw says. "Meet your adoring fans." He makes a wide, sweeping motion toward the crowd.

Taurin shakes his head. His body is still weak, and his mind is exhausted. "No. I'll sit."

Claw's smile turns into something more sinister. His eyes gleam with blue flecks. "I'm afraid you don't have a choice. You see, my friends are anxious to meet you." Over a dozen men wearing dark helmets and tailored suits with pleated pants that tuck into their black boots emerge from the mob. A red *WF* is stitched on their jackets.

Taurin's heart skips a beat. "Watch Force," he breathes.

"Yes. I'm soon to cash in a very valuable reward," Claw says, smirking.

"You said you needed my help."

"I am a liar, a killer, and a thief. You're nothing more than a means to keep my little kingdom alive."

"But you're like me." Taurin points to his eyes. "Organic."

"Ha!" Claw laughs once more. "You are far more valuable to the Seer than I am." The bald man looks toward the approaching patrolmen. His brow sags and his smile turns down into a scowl. "It's a cruel world, boy. You'll know that more than most by the time this is all done." He turns and disappears into the frenzied crowd.

The patrolmen move in around Taurin with steady, even steps, aiming their silver-barreled heat rifles at him. They use no words, but the message is clear: *Come with us.*

Shrift takes a step forward, his anger evident in his expression. "This is all my fault; I brought you here in the first place. I have to do something," he whispers. "They'll kill him."

Violet grips Shrift's arm, pulling it hard. "They'll kill you if you try anything. Be patient." She opens her fist just wide enough to reveal a small, clear object pulsing in her palm, then looks over her right shoulder, searching for something.

"What you got there?" Shrift squeezes Violet's wrist. "Always secrets with you."

"You're hurting me." Violet twists and pulls against him, but she can't free her hand. "It's not what you think."

Shrift pries her fingers open and takes the object from her. He holds it up and stares at it. Its four smooth sides protect a blinking purple light in its core. "This is some kinda tracker. You signaled the Watch Force?" Shrift steps away from Violet. The object continues to flash in his hand.

"It's not like that. I—"

Before Violet can finish, a blast shakes the ground, throwing the spectators to their knees. The patrolmen struggle to keep their footing and hold tightly to the heat rifles in their hands, searching for any sign of an attack. Flashes of orange and red light up the sky, blinding the mob below.

Taurin spits out a mouthful of sand. The blast knocked the speeder over and sent him crashing to the track. Darkness threatens to overwhelm him, pulling him closer with every second. *Just stay awake*, he tells himself.

A white heat pistol appears just inches from Taurin's face. He hadn't seen the stranger approach in the chaos, and now it's too late to escape. "If you want to live, stay down," a stern voice commands. "This is going to get ugly."

Taurin tries to respond, but he can't. An ocean of shadows has already carried him to a place of sleep and dreams. Whatever madness exists outside his mind is no longer his concern—he's at peace.

CHAPTER 23: IMAGININGS

"WAKE UP!" a male voice booms.

Taurin opens his eyes slowly and finds himself in a square room with stone walls. Two bed mats, filled with wild goose feathers, lie in the center. A lit candle burns on the window ledge, and on the opposite wall, the room's wooden door with a copper handle and matching lock hangs open. *I'm home*, he thinks.

"Get up already."

This time, the voice resonates with Taurin. It's one he's heard thousands of times. "Pulp?"

"Who'd you think it was?" Pulp tousles Taurin's hair. "Come on. You don't want to be late."

Taurin blinks, trying to clear his vision. His brother, though just inches away, looks blurred, unfamiliar. His cheeks sag where they should be tight, and his usually vibrant eyes look empty and cold. "You're not Pulp."

The skin melts from Pulp's body, dripping onto the floor like hot wax. Red flames crackle and burn inside Pulp's white skull. His skeleton hands reach out and take a hold of each side of Taurin's head. "WHO AM I THEN?" the skeleton somehow shouts. "TELL ME!"

"Let go of me!" Taurin yells. "This is just a …"

"Dream?" a calm voice finishes. The stone walls and wooden floors fade away and are replaced with blue skies and green grass. Echo sits perched on a bench in the middle of an open field. Her long, curly red hair flows loose with the breeze. "Come and sit."

Taurin shakes his head. "It always feels so real."

"You caught it sooner this time. That's good." Echo taps the empty space next to her with a silver-tipped fingernail.

Taurin sits. "Why do I have to suffer these nightmares to see you?"

"It's the only way around the Watch Force's hold on my mind. They don't expect me to use such violent images to reach you," Echo says.

"I guess I understand."

"You don't have to understand," Echo says. "You have to listen. I've been trying to communicate with you but haven't been able to break through."

"Sleep isn't something I get much of."

"I assumed as much, but the message I have is urgent. Many of those gathered here have been taken to the cleansing room." Echo pauses. "They moved your brother out of our cell a few days ago and I haven't seen him since."

Taurin grinds his teeth and curls his fingers into tight fists. "Can't you do something?"

"I've done all I can." Echo reaches out and touches Taurin's hand with hers. "We need you."

A pulse of light flashes in front of Taurin. He throws his arms up to cover his face, expecting heat or pain to follow, but it never does. When he lowers his hands, the scene has changed again. No longer is he sitting next to Echo on a wooden bench. Instead, he lies flat on a table and black straps bind his arms and legs. He twists his body from side to side, but the effort is useless. The restraints are too strong. Taurin is trapped.

"Be calm," a shadowed figure says. "You are safe."

Taurin narrows his eyes as he looks at his surroundings for the first time. A single bulb hangs above him, casting a soft, sapphire light on the room. Black and red wires protrude from his body like spider legs. A metal cap, cool against his skin, fits tightly around his head. His mind spins and his heart beats fast in his chest. *Stay calm.*

A metal door at the front of the room creaks open. Through it walk six figures, each dressed in khaki pants and white cotton T-shirts. Around their necks hang necklaces made from braided copper wire. Black canvas straps secure heat rifles and ammo to their bodies, and tan scarves cover their faces. One figure steps forward and removes his scarf, revealing a neatly trimmed gray beard that frames the man's tan face. "Hello, son."

Son. The word swirls in Taurin's mind stirring a memory: sitting in a dark room, drinking a strange liquid, and talking about the Watch Force. Of course he's seen this face before but this time it looks so different. "Who are you?"

"No, I guess you wouldn't recognize me," the man says, stepping closer. "You are used to seeing me with a long beard, cane, and a pair of thick glasses."

Taurin's brow furrows. "Brooks?"

"See?" The man turns to the others. "Powerful *and* smart."

Taurin quickly scans the room. Green vines cover the concrete walls that surround him. The air feels damp on his skin and the smell of wet dirt fills his nose. Metal shelves and cabinets, each filled with crates of scrap metal and supplies, line the room's four walls. "What am I doing here, Brooks? Why do you look so different? Why I am strapped to this table?" Taurin grabs at a handful of wires on his arms but can't quite reach them with his hands strapped down. "And what are these?" Fear makes the crimson flecks shine in his eyes.

"Stay calm," Brooks says. "All of this is for your own good. My friends and I saved you."

"What are you talking about?" Taurin looks at the others. "I've never seen them before. And what have you done with Violet and Shrift?"

Brooks nods, and the five others remove their scarves, revealing the faces of four men and one woman. The men all have gray hair cropped short on their heads. The sole woman's long, gray locks are tied back in an uneven ponytail. Like Brooks, each of their faces are lined with rows of wrinkles. Their eyes are a variety of colors that look tired and old. "We are the leaders of a small group called the Seekers," Brooks says. "Our purpose is what it has always been: to free Cinder from the rule of the Seer."

Smoke climbs from Taurin's wrists and ankles. The smell of burning leather fills the room as his restraints dissolve. Taurin rips the wires and cables from his body and removes the metal cap. Taurin jumps from the table and stands with his hands raised defensively in front of him. "Look, I don't care who you are. I just want to get out of here and find my friends."

Brooks smiles, and his gray eyes beam with delight. "You are so very special." He makes a sweeping motion toward his companions. "Leave us." They each nod and step out of the room. The last man to leave closes the door behind him.

"I don't have time for this," Taurin says, frustrated.

"Care for a drink?" Brooks walks over to a table filled with scraps of electronics and piles of papers. A round green bottle sits on top of a stack of leather books. He reaches for it and presses the top to his lips, taking a long drink. Suddenly, he whips the bottle away from his face and bends over in a coughing fit. "Excuse me," he says when he's calm again. "It's a bit stronger than I remembered." He extends the bottle to Taurin with wrinkled fingers.

"I'll pass. Shrift told me what was in the last stuff you made me drink." Taurin's crosses his arms in front of his chest.

"Deception is required at times, but I do apologize for keeping you in the dark for so long. You see," Brooks pauses, "we needed you to find someone for us."

"I found Shrift already."

"Yes, and you did an excellent job with that." Brooks laughs. "Quite a wild spirit he has."

"Wait. Shrift is here?"

"Yes, of course he is here. My fellow Seekers and I came and pulled you from the chaos in Harbor Town."

"All I remember is an explosion and a heat pistol pointed at my face."

"You collapsed before the real fighting happened," Brooks says, shaking his head. "It was a mess. Wars are not tidy."

Taurin pales, and his eyes fill with worry. "What about Violet?"

Brooks crosses to Taurin and places his hand on the boy's shoulder. "She's fine. She was the bravest of us all. With just her fists and feet, she fought a wild crowd of drug-fueled thugs and Watch Force patrolmen. It looked like a rehearsed dance. Beautiful."

Taurin lets out a long breath he didn't realize he had been holding. He nods and rubs his face with palms as the metal door opens again. "She is special."

"Glad you think so," Violet says from the doorway. She runs over to Taurin and wraps her arms around him in a tight squeeze. Her chin digs into his shoulder and her chest presses against his. "You did great."

A warmth flushes Taurin's cheeks. The moment feels incredible—unbelievable. Just minutes ago he was strapped to a table, and now Violet's arms are stretched around him. "Good to see you too."

Violet steps back and straightens her shirt with her hands. She tucks a stray strand of black hair behind her ear. "Well, I'm just happy you're okay." She turns to Brooks, her expression serious. "Did it work?"

"Did what work?" Taurin asks.

"All this stuff," Violet says, motioning to the wires and screens that fill the room. "Was all of this worth it?"

Ignoring Violet's question, Brooks pulls a long table from the wall. The screeching noise of metal against metal blares throughout the room. Pieced together like a puzzle, seven sections of worn, yellowed paper reveal a stunning hand-drawn map of Cinder. The edges are singed, and red smears blotch the top right corner. "Hand me the tablet," Brooks instructs.

"Where did this map come from?" Taurin asks.

"Many Seekers gave their lives to piece together this map," Brooks says somberly. "The Watch Force want to keep such information from us and now we'll see why."

Violet reaches into the leather satchel slung over her shoulder and pulls out the object her father requests. She walks over and places it on the center of the map and steps away. "Your turn," she says, looking at Taurin.

Without question, Taurin walks to the tablet and places his fingers on the symbols in its center. Blue and green lights twist and swirl under his fingertips before the tablet emits a steady stream of red light onto an area on the northern part of the map. Taurin looks at Brooks. "Is this showing what I think it is?"

Brooks bends down and studies the highlighted section on the map, and his eyes grow wide with excitement. "Of course," he says, shaking his head. "It makes perfect sense."

"So the Watch Force base is there?" Violet points at the map. "By that huge volcano?"

"Ha," Shrift laughs. "That'd be too easy." He stands in the doorway, flashing his white smile. "This bunch of weirdos had me hooked up to some machine for hours just to show 'em what I already told 'em." He shoots Taurin a quick wink. "Looks like you got the same treatment, kid."

Taurin nods, then turns his attention back to the map. "So, this is for real?" he asks, pointing to the map again. At the center of the highlighted area, a massive volcano, its mouth bubbling with lava, anchors a long mountain range. "I have to go there?"

"*In* there." Shrift says, walking over to stand next to Taurin. He claps Taurin on the shoulder in a show of support. "We've gotta go into the belly of the beast, partner."

"Yes, yes. You both need to go," Brooks says, shuffling through objects on a wooden shelf. "You won't survive on your own."

Shrift crosses his arms across his chest. "Beg to differ. I made it out once on my own. I could do it again."

Brooks ignores Shrift and walks over to place a thin plastic card in Taurin's palm. "This should get you into the compound. After that, you will be on your own to find the others."

A lump forms in Taurin's dry, raw throat, and he swallows hard. The thought of dealing with an army of patrolmen isn't easy to process. "Are the Seekers coming with us?"

"Not at first," Brooks says, his tone muted. "We believe only Organics can cross into the compound. It would be suicide for the rest of us who aren't gifted. Once you are inside, however, our hope is that you can find a way to let us in."

"If not?" Taurin asks.

"I think you know the answer to that," Shrift says, squeezing Taurin's shoulder. "Let's get gone."

"Before you go …" Brooks gestures to two black canvas bags on the floor beneath the table that Taurin had been lying on. "It's not much, but inside are a few weapons and some supplies." He rubs his wrinkled fingers against his beard. "I hope it is enough."

Shrift bends down and picks up both bags. Metal clangs against metal inside the packs as he slings them over his shoulders. "Me and the kid don't need much."

Brooks squeezes the bridge of his nose between his thumb and finger. "Years of effort and planning have come to this point, so for all our sakes, I hope you are right."

"I'm going too," Violet says.

Brooks casts her a sympathetic look. "Darling, I'm sorry, but that isn't possible. The entrance keeps out all of those who aren't Organics."

Violet breathes in deeply, exhales, and removes a pair of plastic lenses from her eyes. "Don't freak out." She squeezes her eyes shut tightly. "Clear as ice."

Taurin blinks, and suddenly Violet is gone. His jaw drops open and his eyes grow round in surprise. He looks first to Shrift and then to Brooks. "Did you know?" They both look just as shocked and shake their heads.

As quick as she vanished, Violet reappears, her eyes now colored with brilliant flecks of silver. She runs her fingers through her hair nervously. "Sorry I didn't tell you sooner, Daddy. I didn't want to complicate things."

Brooks steps close to Violet and places his hand on her cheek. "Promise me you will be careful."

CHAPTER 24: NORTH

THE THREE companions rush down a worn roadway toward the northern tip of Cinder, the matching ash speeders they ride stirring up storms of sand and dirt behind them. Ready or not, the giant volcano's boiling lava and violent temper wait for them at the end of the path. *Cindy* is what the people of Cinder call the scalped mountain, but it's been years since anyone dared to get close to her. Until today.

Riding alone on a silver speeder that Brooks and the Seekers gave him, Taurin watches Violet's dark hair twist and snap on the speeder in front of him. She chose to ride with Shrift instead of him, and that's okay. An awkward silence had grown between them after she revealed herself, and Taurin didn't know what to say. In all honesty, he felt a little betrayed. She had been like him this whole time and never said a word. He'd spent hours slouched on her bedroom floor talking about what it felt like to have the flecks burn in his eyes and what it meant to be different. *Why didn't she tell me?*

Violet holds on to Shrift's waist tightly. She chose to ride with him because she knew he'd understand her silence. Talking would just complicate things even further, and she was tired of making things more difficult. That was why she hadn't shared who she really was with Taurin or anyone else—it was too messy. The reveal wasn't how she'd planned it, but now her silver flecks were no longer a secret and that was a good thing. Masking her abilities was exhausting. *No more hiding, she thinks. Time to show them all what I can really do.*

It's early when Taurin, Violet, and Shrift arrive at the base of the volcano. The sun still has hours to shine, and a quiet hush blankets all of Cinder, save for the rumble coming from their idling ash speeders. The travelers are now far away from their homes and Harbor Town's buildings made of metal. This is the northern end of Cinder. It's violent and wild—a forgotten place that no one dares seek out.

"Tighten your bootstraps," Shrift says, turning off his speeder. "End of the road."

Taurin quiets his speeder too and swings his booted leg over the side to stand next to it. Before they left, Brooks fitted the trio in matching Watch Force patrolmen uniforms. Homemade and not quite right, the material bunches where it should pleat and folds where it should lie flat. "We look ridiculous," Taurin says, fidgeting with his disguise. "This is never going to work."

"It only needs to work for a minute," Shrift responds.

"Have a little faith," Violet adds.

Taurin kicks a pile of ash with his boot. "Funny hearing something like that coming from you."

"What's that supposed to mean?" Violet says, climbing off the speeder and crossing her arms.

"It means you should have told me about your flecks. You lied *again*. I feel like an idiot."

"Ha, ha," Shrift laughs. "There's a reason you feel that way, partner."

Violet and Taurin each cast Shrift an angry glance. "Stay out of this!" they say in unison.

Shrift raises his hands in surrender and backs away from the pair. "I'll leave you two *lovebirds* alone." Grinning, he turns and walks toward the base of the volcano.

Taurin stares at Violet quietly for a few moments; he doesn't want to speak first. A mix of fatigue, pain, and outright exhaustion distort any true feelings he has. It's been a long few days, each more complicated and difficult than the last. Now with the finish in sight he feels further from her than ever before. "You should have told me," Taurin says, breaking the silence. His words are soft and steady. "I wouldn't have freaked out."

"It's easy to say that now, but when the silver flecks came, things were different." Violet crosses to Taurin and stops just inches from him. "I was younger and afraid. My father warned me what happened to people who were different, so I pretended to be normal. Then, your eyes changed and life became so crazy that there just wasn't time."

"I should have known. You were my best friend."

Violet reaches out and takes Taurin's hand. Her soft fingers, smeared with dirt and grime, squeeze his cracked, bloody knuckles. "I still am."

In all the years Taurin has spent with Violet, he's never seen her quite like this. Silver flecks dot her deep brown eyes, revealing her true self. A soft smile curls Taurin's lips. "They look good on you."

Without a word, Violet leans in and presses a soft, gentle kiss on Taurin's lips. Her body tingles and her face warms. This is the first time she's been so close to someone with her silver flecks showing. The moment lasts longer than she planned, but there's no need to rush something so perfect. Finally, as all things eventually do, the moment fades and she steps back. "Now you know who I really am."

Stunned and smiling, Taurin replies, "I like it."

"If something smells rank over here," Shrift blurts, "it's the breakfast I just splattered on the ground after watching you two lock lips."

"Jealous?" Taurin asks, grinning.

"Nah. Good for you to get a little love before you enter this place." Shrift points a thumb toward the volcano. "Out here, it's kisses and jokes. In there, it's cryin' and pain."

Violet and Taurin exchange looks, their faces both red with worry. Of course it had been stupid to savor such a perfect moment, to wish that something good could find its place in all this hurt. Here, at the base of the volcano, there is no room for comfort.

"You're right," Violet says. She walks over to Shrift's speeder, takes down one of the black bags, and unzips the satchel, searching for a silver heat rifle and a matching pistol. She slings the strap of the rifle across her shoulder and shoves the pistol's barrel down the back of her pants. "Let's do this."

Shrift shakes his head and flashes a bright smile. "Sure glad you're on our side."

"Want any?" Violet motions to the bag filled with weapons.

"Nah. I've got all I need right here." Shrift pats the wooden handle of his copper-plated heat pistol. "She's got a special job to do. I won't take that from her."

Violet nods. "Taurin?"

"I'm no good with those. Never really learned to shoot. My father promised to teach me, but that was a long time ago." He draws an uneven line in the white ash with his boot.

"Sorry about your dad, kid, but most everyone has lost someone close to them. Time to show these bastards that they kicked the wrong hornet's nest."

Taurin tilts his head to the side and cracks his neck. Crimson flecks ignite in his eyes as he looks at Shrift—focused and angry. "Let's do this."

Two people could not be more different than the young boy Shrift first met in the Wasteland and the warrior that stands in front of him now. "Save that fire, kid. You'll need it."

The ground shakes as steaming lava streams down Cindy's black, stone sides. "She's not happy we're here," Violet says.

"Her and me both," Shrift replies. "You two might want to step back. I can't quite remember how this works. He places his right hand against a nondescript section of stone, triggering a blast of steam, followed by a white light that etches a tall rectangle on the volcano's side. Within seconds, a pair of doors over ten feet tall and the color of thick cream replace the coarse, dark stone. A final burp of air pushes ash into the sky, and then all movement and noise stops.

"Amazing," Violet says. She steps to the doors and places a hand on each one. "They feel so real."

"That's 'cause they are real," Shrift says, stepping back. "More real than the rock they replaced and a thousand times stronger." He shakes his head. "Impossible to crack or break in from the outside."

"Can't you just touch the doors and turn into something that can break them?" Taurin asks. "Like the boulder?"

"'Fraid not. I'm limited to natural stuff like rocks and trees. This stuff here ain't natural." Shrift hammers against one of the doors. Not even a faint knock or clang sounds—just silence. "The only other time I saw stuff like this was inside this hell hole."

"So what's the plan, then?" Taurin asks.

Shrift opens his arms wide and bows in front of Taurin. "Just waiting on you, kid."

Violet shoves Shrift out of the way and stands alone in front of the doors. She studies the structure from top to bottom, raking her fingers against the cool, cream-colored material until she pauses at the center of them. She twists her wrist to the right until her four fingers and thumb on one had fit snugly into five small divots. "Found something," she says, smiling.

"Ain't you the smart one." Shrift walks toward the door as Violet takes a step back. He presses his fingers against the dents and turns his wrist, but nothing moves. His face turns red and the white flecks blaze in his eyes as he contorts his fingers and twists his hand. Still nothing. The door stands rigid and unmoved. "Tough nut to crack."

"I think we all know who can open it." Violet reaches out and takes Taurin's hand, guiding his fingers into the divots. "Do your thing."

A slight nod is Taurin's only response. Somehow, when he saw the doors, he knew how to open them and that he could. He presses his fingers against the door, and the crimson flecks glow in his eyes. That familiar energy pulses under his skin. *Open*, he thinks. At first, the divots glow like rubies. Then they turn a light shade of sapphire. Finally, a hiss of air and a blast of steam erupt from the center of the doors. They slide open with ease and disappear into the onyx-colored stone that surrounds them.

Silence hangs in the air for a few moments as the three companions stare into the opening. This is the moment they've all fought so hard for. The harsh heat of the Wasteland, the cruel games of Harbor Town, and even the deadly blasts of the

Watch Force's heat rifles weren't enough to stop them. They've reached their goal—together.

"Beginning of the end," Shrift says. He reaches down to his hip and unholsters his heat pistol and holds the wooden grip snugly in his wide palm. He steadily raises the pistol and aims it toward the opening. "Hope y'all brought a change of underwear."

"Do you think they know we're here?" Violet asks.

"I think they know everything 'bout everything," Shrift answers. "From the moment you wake until you close your eyes at night, they're watching."

"Surely not in the bathroom. We all know what you do in there," Taurin chimes in, giving Shrift a faint smile.

Shrift slaps a hand over his mouth before a booming laugh can escape him. "Kid's funny after all," he says once he's regained his composure.

"Just have to get to know him." Violet winks, then presses the butt of her heat rifle against her shoulder. Even though a fresh coat of paint colors it silver from tip to base, the weapon still looks old and worn. The Seekers gave the companions what they could, but it wasn't much. "Sure you don't want one?" she asks Taurin. "It could help."

Taurin snaps his fingers and orange flames grow from his palms. He blows on the flames and pushes the fire through the air like a bullet. "I'll be okay."

"Show-off." Shrift playfully nudges Taurin with his shoulder. "Let's just hope your bag of tricks is enough."

"It will be." Violet reaches back and loops her long hair into a tight, black ponytail. The sharp lines of her cheekbones frame her confident eyes. "Ready."

Shrift tightens the strap under his green metal helmet and swallows hard. "This'll be fun," he lies.

CHAPTER 25: ENTER

TAURIN, Violet, and Shrift stand in front of a long, dark hallway, a heat pistol, a rifle, and a handful of flames their only defenses. Each side of the corridor is lined with glass, though it's impossible to see through. Each of the trio was sure their first steps into the compound would sound alarms and bring out herds of armed patrolmen, but instead, they were met with silence and darkness.

"Think they could afford some lights?" Shrift jokes, his voice a faint whisper.

Violet presses a shaking finger against her red lips. Her eyes are filled with fright as she watches three patrolmen turn the corner. Just like the uniforms the trio is wearing, these men have pleated pants tucked tightly into their leather boots. Their dark visors cover the fronts of black helmets, hiding their faces, and a red *WF* marks the front of their pressed suit jackets. Holstered heat pistols hang from their glossy black belts. The patrolmen walk together in perfect stride—each heel hits the glass floor in unison. A line of bright white light follows their steps on the glass ceiling above their heads.

A sharp pain explodes inside Taurin's head, sending him crashing to his knees. With his eyes closed and his teeth clenched, he reaches out and pushes his hand against the wall. A single pane of the thick milk-colored glass moves under his palm and swings open, revealing an empty room. Violet wraps her hand around his wrist and pulls him inside. Shrift follows the pair and closes the door behind him. "I feel dizzy," Taurin says, his hands squeezing the sides of his head.

Help, Taurin. Please. The voice, Echo's voice, sounds inside his head. *I know you are close. We do not have time to waste. They are coming for us.*

Taurin drops to his knees again. He can feel a pulse of power growing inside him—a surge of something new. It burns under his skin like the stings from a thousand bees and turns his stomach sour.

"He's bleeding." Shrift points to a stream of blood dripping from Taurin's nose.

Violet places her hands against Taurin's face, her eyes bright with silver. At first her touch is soft, but then she presses her fingers harder against the skin around his nose.

"Stop," she murmurs. "Be still." But the blood doesn't listen to her and just keeps flowing.

"Here," Shrift says, handing Violet a thin white cloth. "Whatever you're doin' ain't working."

Violet grabs the handkerchief and presses it under Taurin's nose. "It's worked before. I mean, it was only a rabbit, but I still stopped the blood and it hopped away."

"'Fraid he's no bunny, and our powers aren't any good in this place." Shrift gestures to their surroundings, sweeping his arms wide above his head. "All this milky glass stops whatever makes us special." He kneels down next to Taurin and studies his face. "Kid got a bit of a buzz is all. He'll be fine."

Taurin nods, the movement slow and forced. "I'm good."

Violet steps back and pulls a small metal disc from her pocket. A purple light flashes from the center of the strange object. "We're close," Violet says.

Taurin blots the blood from his face with the cotton handkerchief Violet gave him. The once-white fabric is now dripping with red. "Close to what?"

"Nothin' good," Shrift says, his eyes fixed on the pulsing disc. "That been doin' that the whole time?"

"No," Violet answers. "This is the tracking device my dad gave me. It's supposed to lead us to my sister, but it's never flashed quite like this before. It might be malfunctioning."

Taurin stands slowly, his knees quivering beneath him. "So we're close to Pulp too?"

"Close to everything, kid." Shrift's white teeth flash in a smile, but the usual humor in his face is lost. Taurin knows that what sits behind these glass walls isn't a mystery to Shrift. As they prepared for their trip to the compound, Shrift had told him about the rooms he'd seen filled with dangling wires and lined with flashing screens. Shrift pulls the copper heat pistol from its holster, and Taurin wonders if he's remembering those rooms now. "This closet won't hide us long," Shrift says. "Better move."

The low hum of Violet's heat rifle vibrates the air. She doesn't want to take any chances and decides to prime the weapon now. Brooks had taught her to shoot at an early age, but not for fun and not as a sport. It was for necessity. *Cinder, after all, is a violent place ruled by a ruthless man and his faceless army,* he'd often say. The phrase meant little to her as a young child; now, she realizes, it means everything.

"Where to?" Taurin asks. "I'm sure the patrolmen are close."

"Rooms like this are all over this place. Not sure what they're for, but there's usually a way in." Shrift gropes the walls. "And a way out." A quick burst of steam scatters dust as the hidden doorway slides open again. "Magic," Shrift mouths.

Violet rolls her eyes and steps past Shrift into the doorway. She looks right and then left but sees only walls of glass. The tracking device throbs in her palm, coloring her skin with shades of purple. She spins around just long enough to give the command, "Follow me," before stepping left into the hall.

The metal disc Brooks gave her to locate Cay wasn't precise, he'd told her as much before she'd left, but it's all he had to give. "The Seekers have access to little technology other than what we can find, barter for, or create," he had told her. "Whatever we do piece together has its limitations."

"If they wanna fight, I'll be ready," Shrift says before stepping into the hallway.

Taurin follows the others and hurries out of the room and closes the door. Drops of red continue to drip from his nose and splatter against the floor, but the pain in his head is too great for him to care. Focus. *Stay alert.*

Minutes pass as the trio makes their way down a long stretch of glass walls. The hallway is silent except for their own breaths and footsteps. The quiet, however, doesn't comfort them; they know it's only a matter of time before silence changes to noise and peace morphs to violence.

Violet presses her back against the wall. "Stop," she whispers. The disc in her palm now emits a dark shade of orange. "I think she's close."

Shrift's breath is shallow as he creeps past Violet and peers around the corner of the hall. He quickly pulls his head back and presses himself flat against the glass. "Gonna need a distraction," he whispers.

Without hesitation, Violet turns the corner and fires a flurry of blasts from her heat rifle. She didn't need to hear what awaited them on the other side. Shrift's eyes told her everything she needed to know, the same way they did the night they battled the Watch Force at Harbor Town. He saw then what she could do with a weapon. She wouldn't disappoint him now, either.

When the trio turns the corner, Taurin sees the bodies of four patrolmen lying limp on the floor just a few yards down the hall. Their tailored suits, now crumpled and unkempt, smoke from the rifle's furious blasts. Two copper-plated doors, each stretching over nine feet to the ceiling, stand behind the pile of bodies. To the right of the doors, a square panel flashes a red light.

"That's one way to cause a distraction," Shrift says.

"You could have warned me," Taurin complains. "I mean, you just turned and fired."

"I didn't have time to get your approval."

"'Fraid we ain't got time for a lovers' quarrel right now." Shrift points to the doors. "That pretty red light is gonna bring the party to us in about a minute."

"What do we do?" Taurin asks.

"Catch." Violet tosses a metal object at Taurin. He bobbles it for a second before grabbing it with both hands.

The gray device he holds is less than an inch thick but longer and wider than one of his hands. It weighs more than its size conveys. "What's this?"

"Put it on the doors and find out," Violet commands.

"Do as she says, kid."

"Stop calling me that!" He grinds his teeth together and slams his shoulder against Shrift on his way to the door. He can feel the anger swell inside him. "I'm not a kid."

"Relax, partner." Shrift holds his hands up in surrender. His trigger finger dangles his copper heat pistol. "I'm on your side, remember?"

"Whatever," Taurin mumbles, then looks down at the piece of tech in his hand. When he was growing up, his father taught him the basics about machines, and the rest he learned from trial and error. Even with that knowledge, the thin piece of metal in his hands is still a mystery.

"Hurry up," Violet says, holding her heat rifle against her shoulder. "I hear footsteps."

Taurin nods and pushes the metal object against the center of the two doors. The sound of metal clanking against metal resonates down the hall. "It's stuck."

"That means it's working," Violet says. "Just wait."

The gray device begins to spin, slowly at first but then faster and faster until it almost disappears in a blur. Dark smoke and the smell of roasting metal fills the air as thin cracks splinter the glass walls surrounding the copper doors.

"Better prime that silver beauty in your hands," Shrift says to Violet. "They'll be here before we get through."

Violet drops to one knee and balances her elbow on the other. Her heat rifle fits snug against her shoulder. "Ready."

The girl's movement is so fluid, so practiced, it almost doesn't register with Taurin. This entire journey he's been on the offensive—usually the one to strike first. Now, unarmed, he's relegated to watching his friends defend him and a strange machine cut through copper doors. At least, he hopes that's what it's doing.

Orange flashes of light erupt as the first stun grenade explodes just a few feet in front of the trio. Blinded and set off balance, they each struggle to see anything other than spots. Violet is the first to steady herself and fires a stream of blasts toward the explosion. Shrift follows her lead, unloading his pistol at whatever approaches.

Taurin grips his face with his hands. Searing pain scorches his mind like wildfire. *Help!* Echo's voice screams. *Make them stop!* Blood continues to spill from his nose, splashing against the floor.

A line of Watch Force patrolmen throw grenade after grenade, each more concussive and blinding than the last. They move forward like a line of ants—each footstep in perfect stride. Dark visors block their faces, but the weapons they wield convey their message.

"Kid's hit!" Shrift yells over the blasts. "Blood." He fires more rounds at the approaching army.

Violet glances at Taurin, still firing her rifle. "You hurt?"

Taurin doesn't respond. The pain in his skull is worse than it's ever been before. *Help! Please!*

Violet turns back to the approaching menace. Taurin is wounded, but she knows the only way to help him is by keeping the patrolmen at bay. One after the other, she burns holes through the red *WF* symbols on the patrolmen's jackets.

It's an easy target, and they fall to the ground just like the metal cans she trained with as a young girl. Even still, more patrolmen swarm the halls to take the places of their fallen comrades until her rifle is out of steam. "I'm empty," she shouts to Shrift.

"Me too, sister." A cloud of vapor billows from the barrel of his pistol. "Never seen so many of these bastards."

As if on cue, the remaining patrolmen raise their heat rifles and aim at the trio. The stun grenades were just for effect, for distraction. The real show starts when a single patrolman steps forward and fires his weapon. The shot rips through the air and pierces Violet's chest.

"Ahhh!" she screams and drops to her knees.

A bright light burns down the center of the copper doors. Taurin freezes. He feels the energy, the surge of power under his skin. Rows of patrolmen, their heat rifles armed and ready, take aim. Unafraid, he steps toward them and spreads his arms wide. They were the ones who killed his father, kidnapped his brother, and now they've struck down the last person who cared for him. It's fury, not anger; rage, not fear, that throbs under his skin. He'll make them pay for everything. He'll make them...

CHAPTER 26: THE SEER

"**STOP!**" A powerful voice roars from behind Taurin. "The boy is not to be harmed."

The buzz from over a dozen heat rifles fades at once as the patrolmen lower their weapons and take a step back. One second more and they would have unleashed their fury on the trio, but now they stand stiff and unresponsive. Their faceless helmets stare ahead with rigid precision.

Although his hands are throbbing and his eyes are burning, Taurin turns to face the voice. He's pictured this moment a thousand times in his mind. The monster who took everything from him would feel the pain he caused. Taurin would make sure of that—at least, that was the plan. Reality, however, is never what the imagination desires.

Scattered patches of white hair frame the man's sunken cheekbones. His eyes, glossed with white, sit above his twisted nose. The old man's thin, brittle arms and hands lie across his lap. His legs are atrophied and strapped to a gleaming silver wheelchair. Red and black wires and tubes filled with clear liquid spring from the metal chair likes vines from a tree, each plunging into the man's emaciated skin. "Not who you expected, boy?" the old man asks, his voice graveled and harsh.

Taurin stands silent for a moment. His crimson flecks calm and his fists go limp at his sides. This ancient man is not the monster he envisioned. "Who are you?"

The man coughs several times, and a thick, wet substance splatters the sleeve of his black tunic. "Excuse me," the old man says. "The years have made my lungs heavy."

"Bet you're still well enough to feel this," Shrift says. He shoves Taurin to the side and aims his heat pistol at the old man's head. His grip is steady as he pulls the sickled trigger, and a single burst of light explodes from the barrel and screeches toward the Seer.

The old man raises his hand in front of his face, his paper-thin, wrinkled skin hanging loose on his gnarled knuckles. The pistol blast burrows deep into his palm, then disappears. "You will never learn." Shaking his head, he snaps his fingers. A row of patrolmen step forward and take ahold of Shrift and scoop Violet up off the floor.

"Let them go!" Taurin yells, "or I'll …"

"You'll what?" the old man hisses. "Burn me with your pathetic fire tricks or perhaps bring down my glass walls?" His white eyes gleam with shards of emerald. "Go ahead. Kill us all and be done with it."

Taurin's outstretched hands shake in front of him, his knuckles white. He wants to do just as the old man said and bring down the walls and finally end this nightmare. It would be the easy way out. The phrase *restrain your flames; hold your tongue runs* through Taurin's mind. It was another one of Clue's challenges, but this one, Taurin never completed.

"I am not an evil man," the old man says. "I may have done evil things, true, but I am not those things."

"Tell that to the people you've killed," Shrift spits.

"Quiet him," the old man commands. A patrolman raises his rifle and brings the butt down against Shrift's face.

Shrift smiles, his lips dripping blood and his teeth covered in red. "Ain't nothin' compared to what I'm gonna do to you."

"Take him away," the man says. "And the girl."

"No, she needs help," Taurin pleads, but before he can say another word, Violet and Shrift vanish down the hallway with the patrolmen.

"You have more important concerns right now," the old man says. "Follow me."

Taurin's rage morphs into hurt and confusion. This was supposed to be the moment where he proved all his effort was worth it. He was going to be brave and strong. Instead, the old man is in control.

"I suppose you know who I am."

"The Seer."

"Follow me. I will not ask again."

Slow and steady, Taurin steps into the room with the copper doors. The throbbing in his head has quieted and his nose has stopped dripping blood. Stacked stones form four walls that stretch to a ceiling made of glass. Long planks of dark wood, each hand-sawed and hammered into place, stretch across floor. At the room's center sits a white table, from which countless wires and tubes stretch to a series of flashing screens and buzzing machines. Four men dressed in white robes surround the table, obstructing Taurin's view. It's an old room filled with new things—each looks as though it has a menacing purpose. Taurin shivers.

The silver wheelchair moves without any effort from the old man. It glides against the wooden planks like ice skates on a frozen pond, until it stops next to the white table. "Most see what we do here as cruel. Then again, most are blind." The

Seer curls and straightens a wrinkled finger at Taurin, motioning him to come closer.

Taurin obeys, trying to control his quivering lips and trembling chin. *Be strong. Be brave.* He glances down at the table again. With each step it becomes clearer that the table isn't empty. Someone is lying on top.

"Closer, boy. You need to see what damage you caused."

A girl no older than Taurin lies silent and still on the table, long strands of red hair spill out around her. Dark leather straps pull tightly against her skin, which is the color of fresh snow. The four men dressed in white robes surround her. Each holds a tablet like the one Taurin took from the temple.

"Echo?" The name leaves Taurin's lips without a thought. She looks different than the girl from his dreams, but somehow still the same. He places his hand on her arm. Her skin feels cold to the touch, like ice.

"She gave much to find you," the Seer says. "If only you had revealed yourself sooner, perhaps she could have been saved such pain."

"Sooner?" Taurin's face twists. "I didn't even know you were looking for me until you stole my brother."

"Yes, that was a mistake. I am not perfect." He taps one of the screens with a milk-colored fingernail. On it is an outline of Cinder filled with various colored lights. "These were once many. Spread across our world like colorful stars in the night sky." He presses a button below the screen and the lights disappear. "Now how many do you see?"

"It's dark. I can't see any."

The old man moves his wheelchair closer to Taurin. "That's right. You, boy, are the last of the great lights."

"No I'm not," Taurin says, frustrated. "I'm just a kid looking for his brother. Nothing more."

A cruel smile creeps across the Seer's face, and flecks of emerald shimmer in his eyes. "Very well. Bring him in."

The four men in white robes exit through a wooden door at the right side of the room. Seconds later, they return with a fifth robed figure dragging between them. Dark stains of crimson blot his white robe. Though his head is limp and his face is covered with a hood, Taurin knows in a second who it is. *Pulp.*

Taurin sprints toward the cloaked men. Hot, fierce energy pulses in his hands, and fire burns in his chest. *Let the white-robed men try and stop me. They can throw everything they have at me, and it won't be enough. Nothing will keep me away from my brother. Not now. Not again!*

"Don't let him through!" the Seer screeches.

The four men scramble to unholster heat pistols from under their robes and aim at Taurin. Bursts of energy fly from their tips, scorching the air, but each shot misses its target.

A ball of orange fire swirls and crackles around each of Taurin's hands. Not a shred of blue colors his eyes—only crimson. The ancient stone walls and wooden floors allow his power to build like it never has before. It feels incredible.

The Seer shouts at the group, but the roar of Taurin's fire and the endless blasts from the heat pistols drown him out and fill the room with deafening noise. The old man's graveled voice is no match for the violence.

"MOVE!" Taurin yells at the robed men, his voice full and deep. They don't listen and continue to blast in his direction. *I warned you*, Taurin thinks. "Burn bright the night. Light the sky!" he shouts. Spheres of fire erupt from his hands and explode against the white-robed men. Like dry twigs, their burning bodies crack against the rock walls and fall limp on the floor. Taurin doesn't notice. He stretches his arms out and grabs the hooded figure in front of him. "I've got you."

The stained robe wilts in his arms. No one is inside.

Slow, steady applause reverberates off the room's hard walls. The Seer slams his hands together, each clap louder and more pronounced than the last. "Organics," the old man laughs. "You are all so predictable."

"He was just here," Taurin says, staring at the empty cloth in his arms. "I saw him."

"You saw what I wanted you to see. That is all."

Hot tears prick at the corners of Taurin's eyes. His heart aches in his chest. "I don't understand."

The old man wheels himself over to where Taurin stands, wraps his brittle fingers around Taurin's arm, and squeezes. "This is not a time for tears, boy. Your brother and your friends are counting on you to be strong." His breath is hot and rank as he speaks. "If you fail me, then their usefulness ends. Do you understand?"

Taurin wipes his tears with the back of his hand, catching them before they spill down his cheeks. His eyes, still painted with crimson, stare at the Seer. "What do you need from me?"

"Follow." The Seer turns the wheels of his silver chair toward the other side of the room, pushing himself across the floor with ease. He turns to speak to Taurin but finds that he's still frozen where he'd left him. "I said to follow!" the Seer commands, irritated.

A thousand thoughts dizzy Taurin's mind. Everything is strange and wrong, like one of Echo's dreams, yet he knows this isn't a nightmare that will end when he wakes. He closes his eyes and searches his mind. *Echo? Can you hear me?* He hears no response, just silence. *You asked me to come, and I did. Now I need your help. I need...*

Be brave, Taurin Gray. We need you now more than ever. Echo's voice is calm in Taurin's mind, less strained than before—even peaceful.

Are you alright? I saw you on the table and I was afraid I was too late.

My body is trapped in this room, and my mind is growing weaker by the minute. The old man has tried to steal what I cherish most—my spirit—but he has failed. Do not let him take what you hold most precious. Accomplish what you came to do. Be strong for all who have given so much.

Taurin opens his eyes. "I'll make you proud," he whispers. "I promise."

"I won't ask again, boy," the Seer spits, his sunken cheeks hot with anger. "Follow me or this ends now."

Taurin moves carefully to the other side of the room. The Seer sits to his left, the stacked stone wall stands stiff in front of him. He takes a few deep breaths in his nose and out his mouth and lets his hands hang loose at his sides. "I'm ready."

"For the sake of your friends, I hope so."

THE SEER

CHAPTER 27: DOORWAY

THE SEER presses a wrinkled hand against the stone wall. His eyes glow green and fierce with energy. "Reveal what is lost. Let us see what is hidden," the Seer chants. Then, like leaves from a tree, the gray stones in front of the old man fall to the floor. They don't crack or crumble—they simply vanish.

Taurin anxiously gnaws at his bottom lip. He expected nothing less than a wall vanishing before his eyes, yet still the sight stirs his stomach. He knows that whatever waits in front of him is nothing like what he's left behind. *Be brave*, he tells himself again.

"Know this, boy. What is beyond this room is unlike anything you have ever witnessed. Few know this place exists. Fewer still have been invited inside." The Seer pauses and turns to Taurin. "Everything I have ever done, good or bad, has been for such a moment as this. You are special, Taurin Gray, but do not think that makes you invincible."

"Show me why you brought me here. We're wasting time," Taurin responds, his voice shaky.

The Seer nods. "Yes, time is running short." The black fabric of the Seer's tunic ripples as he sweeps his arm toward the entrance. "After you."

Fierce and wild power pulses beneath Taurin's skin. The feeling reminds him of the first time the crimson flecks appeared in his eyes. They came with heavy sweats and unbearable pain one night while he slept. First, it was just visions of flames, and then searing pain under his skin and deep in his bones. When it happened, he was sure it was the end, that his young life would be over and there was nothing he could do about it. Everyone knew what happened to those whose eyes shimmered: they disappeared, and so did their families. Nothing was the same after that night. Nothing ever would be again.

The Seer wraps his brittle fingers around Taurin's wrist again and squeezes, bringing Taurin back to the present. "You are ready. Step inside."

Taurin cautiously takes a few steps into the room and blinks slowly. Luminous beams of orange, yellow, and blue light swirl and twist. An unsummoned blue flame ignites his fingertips, frightening him. "What's happening?" Taurin asks.

"Careful," the Seer says, now beside him inside the room. "This place pulls from you what you do not ask it to. Look up and see what has brought you here."

Thick, heavy onyx bark covers the base of a colossal tree trunk. Over twenty feet wide and a hundred feet tall, the dark tree stretches the width of the room and sprawls upward into the blue sky. No roof confines the area—just walls of stacked stone. The orange, blue, and yellow lights twist and spin in the center of the trunk. The ground trembles beneath Taurin's feet—his bones rattle under his skin. Of all the things he expected to be here, this scene never crossed his mind.

"Beautiful, isn't she?" the Seer asks. His silver chair glides across the dirt floor as he moves closer to the tree. The brilliant spinning lights paint his face with vibrant colors. "Come closer."

Something strange pulls Taurin toward the massive trunk. Not the Seer's words, no, something else that can't be heard. Something primal, buried deep within him. He stretches his fingers out to touch the onyx bark, but the old man pushes them away.

"Not yet," the Seer says.

Taurin shakes his head and takes a step back, breaking the tree's strange hold on his mind. "What is that thing?"

"The Glowing Gate," The Seer responds. "At least, that is what the first people called it."

"Was it built?"

The Seer laughs. "Such a gate cannot be built, boy. It grows only from an area of its own choice and for whatever reasons, beyond my understanding, this Glowing Gate chose here to rise."

"You keep calling it a gate, but it's just a tree with some lights in the middle. It's a trick," Taurin says, although he knows it isn't true. He can see that what is in front of him is something special. This is no ordinary tree wrapped with blinking bulbs. The spinning lights and their power pull at him as if he was tethered to them. It takes all his strength to resist the urge to touch them.

"Be glib if you like, however, we both know this is no illusion. I too can feel its pull and power. It calls to me, pleading to be locked once again."

"Why don't you?"

The Seer turns his silver chair to face Taurin. His face glows with a thousand shades of orange and blue. "I have tried everything to control this gate. Gathering all of those that might possess its key."

"Organics?"

"Yes. Like this tree, there are those who feed off this world, pulling magic from the sky and the stones, possessing abilities that most cannot imagine." He turns his emerald eyes back to the twisting light. The Seer looks lost for a moment—his face droops with sorrow. "Many have tried to stop the Glowing Gate. All have failed."

"I don't understand. Why lock it?"

Wrinkled fingers pull the robe's black hood down, revealing the Seer's full face. "How old do you think I am?"

Taurin cringes before shaking his head. "I don't know."

"Look at me, boy." The Seer glares at Taurin. "My skin is thin like paper. My bones crack and creak, and my body is kept alive only by tubes from this damned chair. Yes, I am a very old man. Older than you can possibly imagine."

"I believe you. You smell like death, but how does that close this gate and bring my brother home?"

"Watch your tongue!" The Seer spits each word like venom. "You have no idea what waits beyond this gate and all I've done to protect my people."

"You have no people," Taurin says, his words pointed and harsh. "Whatever world you once controlled has slipped through your fingers. Armed men steal children from their beds at night and murder those who did nothing wrong. For years, you and your band of masked thugs have tormented our world, and for what? To control a stupid gate?"

The Seer drops his chin to his chest. His eyes, now clouded and dim, look down at the dirt that covers the ground. The fierceness that pulsed through his body fades and he suddenly looks much older than before. "I was among the first to settle this world. I was tasked with keeping those who were sent here from ever leaving. You see, this world of fire and stone is a special kind of prison. And I was appointed its warden."

"No way. You'd be—"

"Hundreds of years old?" the Seer interrupts. "Yes, that is true. My people have unlocked many secrets. That is why, I suppose, we have fought so many wars." He reaches to the side of his chair with shaking, unsteady hands and pulls a transparent tablet from a protective sleeve. "Come here."

Taurin walks over to the old man and looks down at the now-glowing object in his hands. On it a blue and green sphere, tilted to one side, spins. "What is that?" Taurin asks.

"Not *what*, boy. *Where*." He hands the tablet to Taurin. "Place your palm on it."

"I have a bad history with these things."

"If you want to see your friends and your beloved brother alive, you will do as I ask."

Taurin stares at the screen in his hands, studying the twisting sphere. *Violet would love this*, he thinks. Of course she would; she enjoyed anything new and different. That's why he went to the temple so many nights ago—to impress her. She was always so smart and in control. Just once he wanted to be the one to discover something new and teach her about it. He wanted to be the one in control.

"Go on," the Seer commands. "We have no time to waste."

Taurin flattens his fingertips against the screen. The brightly colored sphere grows to twice its original size before turning black under Taurin's hand. "I think it's broken."

"Patience, boy. Wait and see."

Taurin pulls his fingers away from the tablet. "Whatever this is meant to show me isn't working. I'm done."

The Seer clicks on the screen with a single fingernail. "Look again. Tell me what you see."

"This is a waste of time," Taurin says, but he glances down at the tablet once more. His blue eyes grow wide as he studies the screen. The black sphere is now covered with a rainbow of colored flecks. "This isn't Cinder."

"No. It is not."

Taurin can feel his heart race. Droplets of sweat form on his brow and drip down his cheeks like rain. Something is special about this sphere filled with flashing lights—he can feel it. "Where is it?"

The Seer sighs and rubs the soft skin on the side of his head. "It's called Earth."

A violent explosion shakes the ground and rattles the stone walls. Dark smoke fills the space and soars up toward the top of the mighty tree. Taurin drops to the dirt and covers his head with his arms. The Seer, still confined to his chair, can only shield his face. Bits of rock burst in every direction as countless blasts of light slam against the walls.

"Stay down!" a voice yells. "We're coming to get you!"

Deafening explosions continue to rattle the ground and shake the stones from the sides of the room loose. Taurin can taste dirt in his mouth, but he doesn't care. He'd burrow down deep into the dank soil if he could to escape the confusion.

"Fools!" the Seer yells. "You will kill us all!"

"Not *all*," a gruff voice replies. "Just you." Sunlight reflects off the barrel of a copper heat pistol as Shrift slips into the room. His eyes are black and swollen, and he glares at the old man. Smears of fresh blood flow from open wounds on his face, but he grins, triumphant.

"You're pathetic," the Seer spits. "Cinder will burn to ash and for what? The life of one boy?"

"'Fraid you won't be around to see it either way." Shrift closes his left eye and aims with his right. "Sometimes an animal just needs to be put down for his own good."

Taurin looks up just in time to see the blast from the pistol tear through the Seer's chest. Part of him wants to cry out and stop Shrift, but the rest knows it's too late. The deed is done. His friend has done just as he promised. If the Seer was once a powerful man, he doesn't show it at the end. He utters no final threatening words or attempts a last stand. The old man just slumps over and topples to the ground.

Dozens of men and women fitted with worn khaki pants and drab green helmets fire blast after blast from their handmade heat rifles. The Watch Force patrolmen never expected such an attack, especially from the Seekers. The small army of gray-haired soldiers, led by Brooks, fires at the Watch Force until every last tailored jacket and black helmet lies motionless on the ground.

"It's over," Brooks says, extending his hand to Taurin. "Time to stand up and see your future."

The leather feels good against Taurin's palm, soft and comforting. He grips Brooks's glove tightly and allows himself to be pulled from the dirt. Black smoke still billows toward the top of the hulking tree; the spinning lights beam and swirl at its center. "Nothing has changed."

Brooks smiles. "Oh, I wouldn't quite say that. Look over there at the doorway."

Time slows as Taurin turns his head. At first, his brain dismisses what his eyes see as a trick, another illusion. After a moment, however, he knows that it's different this time. The man standing there with broad shoulders, a square jaw, and tufts of brown wavy hair can only be one person. "Pulp!"

CHAPTER 28: CHOICES

DARK smoke rises, debris litters the floor, and bodies lie all around the room. The fallout after the battle matters little to the brothers. It has been a long time since they have seen each other—too long.

"Good to see you, *Mouse*," Pulp says, tousling Taurin's hair. Mouse was a name Pulp had given Taurin when they were much younger. Taurin had always been the small one, the runt, so the nickname just fit. At first, Taurin's brother had used it to tease him, but somewhere along the way it changed to mean something more. If anyone had a problem with Mouse, they knew they had a problem with Pulp too.

"Wasn't sure I'd make it," Taurin says, his voice guarded.

Pulp curls his arm around his brother's neck and squeezes. "I never doubted you."

"I did, every day. I worried that no matter what I did, it wouldn't be enough." Taurin scans the room and shakes his head. "It almost wasn't. I mean, look at this place."

"Wouldn't fret about it too much. This place was bloody and violent long before you showed up." Pulp looks down at the floor. "Dad would've been proud of you, Mouse. I know I am."

"So you heard?"

Pulp nods slowly, pointing at the Seer's body. "He made sure I knew what happened. Never seen someone as cruel as him. Young or old, it didn't matter. If they had something he wanted, he just took it. We're all better off now that he's gone."

"There's a lot of ugliness in this place." Taurin pauses and takes a deep breath. "We've seen things we wish we could forget."

"True, but there's beauty too." Pulp nudges Taurin with his elbow. "I think she's looking for you."

Violet's raven hair, no longer pulled back, flows freely down her back as she searches the room. Her hands perch on her hips in fists as her dark eyes, flecked with silver, scan the area. It takes only a second for her to find who she is looking for, and even less time to cross the room to get to him. "I thought you were dead," she says, wrapping her arms around Taurin.

"He might be soon if you keep that up," Pulp laughs.

"Pulp!" Violet squeals. Her arms are too small to stretch around his massive shoulders, but she tries anyway. "It's so good to see you. I'm so glad you're safe."

"Me too," Pulp says, pulling away and lowering his eyes to the floor again. "Not everyone was as lucky."

Violet shakes her head. "No. You're wrong." Sweat beads on her brow and drips down her red cheeks. "She's here. I know it."

"I'm sorry, Violet." Pulp says. "Cay is gone."

Silver flecks burn brightly in Violet's eyes. Fury and sorrow throb in her chest and itch to be let out. She longs to strike Pulp down for lying, to show him her true powers, but in her heart she knows he's telling the truth. Cruelty won't bring Cay back—nothing will. It takes energy to be strong and stoic, and she has none left. She gave every ounce of it to the journey—to the fight. Silent, she slumps to the floor and vanishes.

Pulp eyes widen. "Where did she go?"

Taurin presses a finger to his lips. "Give her time," he mouths to Pulp.

Invisible and away from the rest of the world, Violet weeps. She presses her forehead against her knees and rocks back and forth. It's painful to accept that Cay's life was cut short by the Seer or his men. *A sister should have known*, she thinks. Even a sister who wasn't aware she was one until recently.

Cay was her father's secret, hidden away like a jewel or a prize. Her eyes shimmered too, and that was dangerous. Brooks had told Violet that, because he knew what happened to those who were special, he had hidden her sister away in the hope that it would keep her safe. It didn't. The Seer had found her and taken her from her hiding place. That's when Violet learned she wasn't her father's only child.

At first Violet had been angry at her father for keeping her in the dark for so many years, but that anger turned to hope when Brooks tasked her with bringing Cay home. After all the years apart, they would finally have the chance to be together—to be a family.

The memory is too much to contain, and Violet's body flickers and flashes until she is no longer invisible. Taurin reaches for Violet and pulls her to his chest. It's unfair, he knows, that Pulp sits just inches from him and Cay is gone. Nothing he can say could make this moment any easier, so he stays quiet and just holds her as she sobs into his chest. Even with all his abilities, Taurin feels powerless to do anything to change the past.

"I'm so sorry, my darling," Brooks says. "I failed you both."

"No," Violet says, wiping her tears with her hand. "You did your best. We all did."

Father and daughter embrace for a long while. "It's good you are all here," Brooks says. "The time for grief will need to be put on hold, I'm afraid. Many have lost much today. But to stop now would disgrace their memories." He stretches his arm out and takes Violet's hand. "We must discuss the gateway."

Pulp and Taurin turn to the ancient tree. The glowing, spinning lights paint their faces with hues of green and blue. "What does this thing have to do with us?" Taurin asks, skeptical. The Seer had started to explain things before Shrift ended that conversation abruptly. "And where is Shrift?"

"He is busy at the moment," Brooks answers. "What I am about to tell you is something he is already aware of."

"Daddy, what is going on?" Violet asks.

"Please, I know you all have questions, but you have to let me speak for a few moments." Brooks reaches into his pocket and takes out a worn leather notebook. Black and cracked, the book is both smaller than the palm of his hand and twice as thick. Hundreds of yellowed pages are filled with symbols and words, each written or scribbled by hand. "My life has been devoted to this book. Violet can attest to that."

"What's inside?" Pulp asks.

"Centuries of secrets," Brooks says and then turns his attention to Taurin. "What did the Seer tell you before the explosion?"

"He wanted me to close the gate." Taurin points to the swirling light at the center of the tree. "He told me I was the only one who could do it, but he didn't say why."

Brooks flips through the leather notebook and then rips a tattered page from it. He scans the handwritten letters for a few seconds and then places the paper in Taurin's hand. "Read what this says."

Taurin clears his throat and rubs his chin with his fingers. Two words are all that's written on the scrap of paper. However, he can feel that these eleven letters hold a greater meaning than an entire library of books. "World walker," he reads aloud.

The glowing gate throbs brighter, its twisting lights spin and bark rumbles with a veiled energy. The room's stone walls rattle and shake once more, cracking the dirt beneath the tree's colossal trunk. "This can't be good," Pulp says.

Brooks grabs Taurin's shoulders and stares into his eyes. "I have spent my entire life uncovering the secrets of our world and have lost much because of that pursuit. So trust me when I tell you that you possess a gift so exceptional that it will quite literally change everything."

"You're starting to freak me out," Taurin says.

"You should be freaked out, partner," Shrift says from the doorway. "I'm sure that whatever's behind that gate is just a whole lot of pain and misery. Why else do you think that old bastard did so many terrible things to try and close it?"

Taurin sees a movement beside his friend and catches a glimpse of a strand of red curls. Echo moves to stand beside Shrift, her green flecks shimmering like stars in her eyes.

"More than terror waits beyond that gate. I've felt it," Echo says.

"Am I the only one who doesn't know who she is?" Violet asks, gesturing to Echo. "Want to fill me in?"

"No time for that right now, my dear," Brooks says. "We must remain focused." The ground trembles once more, this time more violent and jarring. "The moment has finally come."

His face pallid, Taurin turns his gaze to the glowing gate. Bright lights swirl in the black bark. If it wasn't terrifying, it might be beautiful. "Why me?"

"The answer to that question is one you must discover for yourself," Brooks says, his eyes wide and wild with excitement. "You have been given the ability to cross worlds. According to my research, such a power hasn't been seen in Cinder for hundreds of years. Use it, son. See what is beyond the sand and grime that covers Cinder. Explore it."

Taurin shakes his head and, with a cracking voice, says, "It's not that easy. I mean, I just got my brother back and now I'm supposed to leave him again? That's not how this was meant to end." Frantic, he looks to Violet for support. "Tell him that this is crazy. Tell him he's wrong!" The room rumbles, sending blocks of stone crashing to the ground.

Violet, unfazed by the chaos around her, steps to Taurin and takes his hand. "I can't tell him that because he's not wrong. You were made for this. We all know it."

"She's right, Mouse. Dad would want you to go," Pulp says. Even if it meant leaving everything else behind."

"Can't you all come with me?" Taurin pleads.

"The Seer tried to accomplish that for years and failed each time," Brooks says. "It cost many innocent lives. I am sorry, but it has to be only you."

Echo pushes through the crowd surrounding Taurin. Her voice is soft and gentle when she speaks. "That's not true. The gate can support him and others like him once it has been opened."

"And you know this how?" Brooks asks, his eyes narrow.

"My gift is that of sight. The Seer may have used that gift for his purposes, but by doing so, I was able to look into his own mind and see the truth. Once Taurin opens the gate, he and other Organics can cross."

"What if you're wrong? What if—"

Shrift thumps a thick finger against Brooks's chest, stopping his words. He grins, flashing his white teeth. "She ain't wrong and you know it."

"Everyone just back off for a second. I need to think." Taurin shuts his eyes tight and focuses on the darkness. The ground shakes beneath his feet, and stones continue to crumble from the walls. Whatever is happening can't be stopped—he knows that now. This journey that has spread the length of his entire world has to continue. There is no other choice. His eyes, glowing with crimson, look to his friends. "Are you sure enough about what you say to step through the gate with me, Echo? Do you really trust that I'm strong enough, Violet? Do you ..."

"Let me stop ya right there," Shrift interrupts. "I'm goin' with you, and ain't nothin' gonna stop me."

"Me too," Violet says, smiling.

Echo nods. "It is meant to be."

"Pulp?"

"No flecks for me, Mouse, and that's okay. Plenty of work to do here now that the Seer is no longer in charge. Lots of people will need help. Dad would want me to stay."

Taurin throws his arms around his brother. "I'll miss you."

"Me too," Pulp says, squeezing Taurin tightly. "Just remember what Dad always told us—be brave."

"I will. I promise."

"Be safe, my darling," Brooks says and kisses Violet on the cheek. "I raised you to be strong. You have learned the rest on your own. I am so very proud."

"I love you, Daddy."

"And I love you. Always."

"Ah-hem," Shrift clears his throat. "Hate to break up this special moment, but we got to get going."

"Yes, of course," Brooks blurts. He reaches into his pocket, pulls out a rolled piece of yellowed paper, and passes it to Taurin. "Read what this says aloud. If my study is correct, it should open the gate."

"That's it?" Taurin asks.

"It will have to be my final *clue* for you, my boy." A knowing smile covers Brooks's face, and he winks. "Good luck."

Taurin unrolls the paper and, after a few long breaths, reads the handwritten words aloud. "Unlock what is bound. Shine light on the darkness."

In an instant, the room stops shaking and everything falls silent. The vibrant whirling lights morph and transform into an arched, glowing doorway. Without a word, Taurin, Violet, Shrift, and Echo join hands and step forward into the light. The companions will need to be strong. They will need to be fearless because what lurks on the other side of the light is a danger unlike anything they've ever faced. As they step through the gate, Taurin reminds himself of what his father always said.

Be brave.

Be BRAVE.

BE BRAVE!